THE SECRET OF GIDON

BOOKS

ELIZABETH REVILL

The Secret of Gidon
Published in 2021 by
AG Books
www.agbooks.co.uk

Distributed worldwide by
Andrews UK Limited
www.andrewsuk.com

Contents

Acknowledgements

I would like to thank Joe Larkins and everyone at Andrews UK for making this happen, Jeff Jones for proofreading and especially, Yvonne Macevoy for her delightful illustrations. I couldn't have done this without you, Yvonne.

for Chloe & Daniel, Scarlett & Rose

1: Lazy Summer Days

It was one of those days when nothing much was happening on the streets. School had broken up for the summer and those children lucky enough to go away all seem to have chosen the same week for their holiday.

Trevor scraped his already scuffed and dusty shoe along the side of the crumbling brick walls belonging to a row of condemned terraced houses on the opposite side of the road to where he lived. He screwed up his face as his heel caught on a chip of stone, which screeched over the pavement. The sound made him shiver, in just the same way as if a fingernail had been scratched down a blackboard.

Trevor stopped at an old worn stone front door step. He was bored. Jacko, Beany and Muffin, his three friends from Factory Street had gone to the reservoir to look for frogs but Trevor's mother had kept him at home to run errands and help her in the house. He'd cleared the back yard, swept the entry and been to the paper shop for her. Now she'd gone to work. He stared at the three single pound coins and two fifty pence pieces in his grimy hand. He put the two fifty p's together and counted the sides of one coin. There were only seven. He thought there would be more. Then he noticed his chewed and broken fingernails and shamefacedly slipped the money into his back pocket with a sigh.

The four pounds were for fish cake and chips for his lunch, his mother had said, but he wasn't feeling very hungry. Several thoughts passed through his head. He could buy some fags. Mr. Clinton at the corner shop sold them separately from under the counter and away from view. His mother said it was to help those people who were short of cash. Trevor secretly thought if they couldn't afford it they shouldn't smoke. But, then what did he know?

He'd always wanted to try and smoke a cigarette just once. He was curious to see what it was like but then again that wouldn't be any fun without his friends and he'd need an older boy to buy them for him. That could bring its own problems. Nah! Smoking was a mugs' game. It was a bad idea.

He pulled on his front door key, which was on a chain around his neck, swinging it from side to side, feeling each link move against his skin.

There wasn't even anything worth watching on the television. He paused and kicked idly at the already splintered door, in front of him, daubed with chalk and paint. It creaked open and the damp, musty smell of the old house crept up his nose.

"Trevor! Trevor!" called a voice from the end of the street.

Trevor looked back. It was Suki. What did she want? She wasn't bad, as girls went, but she was still a girl.

"What?" Trevor yelled back at her.

"Do you fancy a game or something?"

"Nah!"

It would be just his luck to start playing with her and for Jacko or Muffin to turn up and see him with her.

Suki came running up.

"Oh, go on. I'm really fed up. My mum's gone shopping and said I had to stay here."

Trevor sat on the step and picked at the warm tar bubbles oozing in the gutter with a piece of stone.

"There's nothing to do – besides I wouldn't ask you to play if anyone else was here."

"Oh no?"

"No! You don't play fair at..." She stopped and squealed loudly.

"What's the matter?"

"A rat, there's a rat in there. Shut the door!"

Trevor smiled wickedly, "Tell you what, you go in and stay there for a count of ten and I'll play with you."

"No chance."

"Ah well, that's that!" said Trevor with a wry smile.

"It's not the rat although they scare me but it's number nineteen"

Trevor turned. In his boredom he hadn't taken any notice of the number of the house he'd sat outside. A Mrs. Bosworth had lived there. She was a strange old lady whom the children had labelled a witch. No one had ever been inside her home even after she'd left and moved to a new flat for old people. There were many rumours and stories about this property, so much so, that even before this side of the street had been condemned, no one had lived on either side of number nineteen for many years.

"That's funny, I thought the door was locked. Me and Jacko tried it once when, when she first left but we couldn't find a way in what with all the windows boarded up and that; we could only look through the letter box and then we never saw anything." Trevor paused for a moment, "Tell you what, you come in here with me and have a look around and I'll play with you."

Suki shook her head, "I don't know. I don't fancy the idea at all."

"Aw, come on," urged Trevor. He was feeling a little excited at the thought of entering this spooky domain as well as a little frightened.

"Well, just for a minute then. Only let's go and get some matches or something first so we can see."

"Nah! There's enough light from the door to see what we want. Come on!" Trevor stood up and brushed the gravel and dust from his jeans. "Come on!" he insisted.

"Oh, I don't know Trev," murmured Suki uncertainly.

"I said, come on," hissed Trevor. He grabbed Suki by the hand and dragged her into number nineteen.

Once inside it was like a different world. The musty smell of damp was all around them and the house was so quiet that Factory Street seemed a million miles away. The rays of sunlight gave the place a twilight look, hardly piercing the gloom of the old living room. The wallpaper was torn and peeling. In one corner was an over turned splintered wooden chair, which was long past repair. As Trevor moved forward, a rat with half a tail scuttled past, out towards the kitchen and the back yard.

On a wall near the stairs stood a large grandfather clock, covered in dust, but amazingly enough, still ticking.

"Hey Suki! Look at the size of that!"

"It's a bit different from our electric wall clock at home," said Suki. "It's strange, you know. I thought I'd hate it, coming in here but, I feel ... well, sort of at ease."

"Yes, I know what you mean," replied Trevor. "Shall we have a proper look round?"

As the two children stumbled over a piece of rotting carpet and moved towards the back room and kitchen the little sunlight that had crept in was suddenly cut off. Trevor and Suki both turned to see that the front door had shut quite tight and had bolted from the inside.

"How the....?" murmured Trevor.

He picked his way over to the door and tried to slide back the heavy bolts but they wouldn't give, not even a little.

"But how?" was all Suki could manage to say. She thumped hard on the boards covering the windows. "Trev... we're going to be stuck here for ages. There's no one about and won't be for hours."

"Don't be silly," said Trevor, "There's a back door, isn't there? That'll be easier to open and there's an upstairs. Those windows aren't boarded up. Don't worry, failing all else, we can probably push out the boards that cover the windows here."

"But you said, you and Jacko tried and couldn't get in."

"Yeah, well we didn't try that hard."

"I just don't understand it that's all."

"Look, if you're feeling frightened, go upstairs. It'll be light in the rooms up there facing the street. Just shout when you see a grown up or someone. They'll get us out, but let me try the back door first, all right? We don't want to look complete idiots. Okay?"

"Okay, Trevor," agreed Suki and she started to feel her way towards the stair door.

"Trev...or...!"

Trevor noticed a tremor in Suki's voice as she called his name.

"Trevor, the door, the door on the grandfather clock... it's opening." Her voice wavered uncertainly.

Trevor edged closer to Suki and watched as the clock door swung to against the damp, cracked wall. From inside the clock came an eerie blue light, which pervaded the room.

"Look," said Suki. "There are steps inside the clock, going down. Shall we go and see? I'm feeling okay again, honestly."

"I don't know. I don't much like the idea of the clock door shutting on us as well. Let me just check the back door."

"Oh, come on. Look, there aren't any bolts on this door. It can't lock behind us."

And before Trevor could call her back, Suki had stepped down inside the clock and was starting down the old steps.

"Wait for me!" called Trevor and he too, made his way inside the timepiece from a bygone era and began to climb down the roughly hewn stone steps.

The rocky walls on either side shone with a phosphorescent glow. After they'd tiptoed down about seventeen steps the descent became much steeper and soon the sound of water reached their ears.

"Ugh! We're just coming to a sewer or something," grumbled Suki, her nose wrinkling in distaste and her voice came echoing back to her.

"I don't think so," muttered Trevor. "Anyway, it won't hurt to see, will it?" His voice was barely a whisper as he moved on.

"I suppose not. We've come this far. Anyway, I've never seen a sewer."

"What do you know about sewers?" hissed Trevor scornfully, "Tell me that!"

"Not a lot," said Suki confidently, her voice getting louder. "Only what we've been taught in school about the Victorian age." Suki suddenly came to a standstill.

"What now? asked Trevor.

"I can see lights, dancing lights. Look Trev."

There in front of the children the steps opened out into an underground cave and directly opposite to where they were standing was a tunnel, which appeared to be lit by a myriad of tiny flickering lights.

"What are they?" asked Suki.

"I don't know," said Trevor, "But look over there!"

Suki followed his finger, to the left of them was a small rocky ledge running down to some water. The water was lapping gently around a small coracle, which was moored to that ledge.

"See the water goes right through the tunnel of dancing lights," said Suki. "Let's take the boat and see where it leads."

"Hold on," grumbled Trevor, "We could keep following paths, canals and tunnels all afternoon and never get anywhere."

"You're not backing out? Now, who's the scaredy cat!" exclaimed Suki.

"No, I'm just being sensible. We don't want to get lost."

"Okay. Fair enough," agreed Suki. "Let's just try going down this tunnel in the boat and I promise you, if there's a fork or any more tunnels running from this main one, we'll come right back. The water's not flowing that quickly, it should be easy. I don't fancy getting lost either."

"Right! It's a deal. Spit and shake?"

"Spit and shake," nodded Suki and spat on her fingers. Trevor did likewise. They slapped their hands together and sealed their bargain.

The two children walked carefully to the ledge and Trevor held the small coracle close to the side until Suki was safely inside the boat. He quickly untied the rope from the end of the iron stake and then Suki secured the boat as tightly as she could while Trevor climbed in.

2: The Adventure Begins

Trevor picked up the small paddle and scooped it through the water, first one side then the other, just as he had seen the canoeists do on television and films. Just as they approached the mouth of the tunnel, a strong current seemed to come from nowhere. It caught the boat and swung it around. It tugged and pushed it at a tremendous pace down the tunnel of dancing lights. The two children clung to the sides of the coracle with both their hands and Trevor lost the precious paddle from his grasp.

"Hold on, Suki!" called Trevor and closed his eyes tightly as the rocky walls came dangerously close to the little boat.

"I can't see where we're going!" screamed Suki. "We just seem to be going down deeper and deeper."

"Look out, Suki! Duck!" shouted Trevor.

Suki lowered her head, just in time, as the ceiling of the rocky tunnel dropped down dramatically leaving very little headroom.

Travelling at such a speed had the effect of making the dancing lights look like small explosions, diving and zooming towards them. Then, just as suddenly as the current had caught them, the water returned to its previously calm condition and the small coracle floated out into a large rocky cavern and came to rest at the foot of some steps where a man was standing.

He was tall and thin with silvery grey hair, which grew from a peak at the top of his forehead and receded back at either side of his temples. His hair tumbled freely down onto his shoulders. His eyebrows were finely arched giving him a quizzical expression. His eyes were large and grey, emphasising his lean, gaunt face. He had a classical aqualine nose and his thin lips were drawn tight across his neat, white teeth in a welcoming smile. His chin was covered with a wispy goatee beard. He was dressed, from head to toe, in a long, black cassock like garment. He released his hands from their clasp in front of him and stretched them out towards the two children.

"Welcome, Suki! Welcome, Trevor!" He nodded to each child, "Come take my hands."

His voice was warm, rich and relaxing to listen to. The children did as he asked and jumped up the granite steps.

"I have been waiting for you, but I thought you would have been here much sooner," said the melodic voice of the stranger.

"You mean we were expected?" said Trevor, amazed.

"How did you know our names? How did you...?"

"Ssh," smiled the old man stopping Suki's excited questioning. "This will explain much."

He stretched out his left hand again. On his little finger was a large, opalescent ring, which he asked the children to look into, as they did so, they saw a perfect image of the front room of number nineteen, the grandfather clock and the door leading into Factory street. The only movement in the room now was that of the scuttling rat, which the children had seen earlier.

"So, that's how you knew we were coming. But, what about the front door bolting behind us and the grandfather clock?" asked Suki.

"Yeah, and how come the door to number nineteen was open in the first place?" queried a puzzled Trevor.

The questions came tumbling out one after the other. The man quelled them all by raising his ivory hands.

"Please, please; one at a time. I know you are curious and I will try to answer as many of your questions as I am able, but only when the time is right. Put your trust in me."

"We can't do anything else," said Suki disdainfully.

The elderly man smiled again and spoke with authority, "I am Manovra, master of all. I am the guide of the dwellers of the Inner Earth and I need your help. But your help must be given of your own free will or it will be of no use. If you decide not to aid us I will have to start a search for someone else to save my world." Manovra spoke with a quiet dignity, which immediately commanded the respect of the children.

Somehow, they felt they could trust him. They knew he wasn't a bogeyman come to whisk them away from their families. They knew he was a good wise man and they felt no fear.

Trevor answered without any hesitation, "I'll help you, sir." And he looked across at Suki whose face broke into a toothy grin.

"So, will I."

"Good, it is good," nodded Manovra, "Come take my hands and I will take you to Gidon and try to explain all that is to be done. Come!"

The children looked up trustingly at Manovra, took his offered hands without hesitation and began to ascend the granite steps.

As they walked Manovra's mellow voice unfolded an amazing tale about how he had started a mammoth search for a human being with the necessary qualities to save his land.

Apparently, as long as Mrs Bosworth lived at number nineteen there was no danger to Gidon because she was a friend to Manovra and his people. She possessed the virtues needed to weave the magic and cast the spell to renew the enchantment on the fountain of ice.

"The fountain of ice is situated in the Hall of Whispers. It contains a crystal, which is Gidon's source of energy. It provides light, warmth and reacts with the lumigles, they being the little creatures on the walls of the tunnels, which look, as you so aptly put it Suki, like dancing lights, to give us water," explained Manovra. "When a piece is broken off, to be used somewhere in Gidon, from the break will come a rain like spray. Only when the fountain is once more in liquid form and all the magical crystal power used, can the enchantment be renewed to return it to a fountain of ice once more. It also has restorative powers to heal so there is no sickness in the land."

"Cor!" said Trevor his eyes wide with wonder.

"The crystals have other magical properties, too numerous to mention, and the enchantment can only be placed on the fountain by a human being who can plant a kiss of innocence on the fountain wall, join hands in friendship over the stone-work, promise secrecy and to return again when they are summoned," continued Manovra. "That's where you come in."

"Sounds easy enough," said Trevor.

"A doddle," agreed Suki.

"Ah, but there is more, much more." intoned a sombre voiced Manovra.

They finally reached the top of the steps they had been climbing and in front of them stretched a large cavernous chamber with many passages and caves leading off.

"Whew!" said Trevor. "That's quite a climb."

"Where are we?" asked Suki in wonder.

"This," said Manovra, "is the Cave of the Shifting Sands. The sandy floor is slowly revolving. If you stand still you will feel yourself being moved around. It turns for our protection. Only one of these passageways leads to Gidon. Unless you belong there or are a friend to us, you will never find the way. You could wander these passages for all eternity, facing untold dangers. You would be surprised at just how quickly you can lose your bearings, especially as the cave alters the way it is turning at random intervals."

"Surely, someone could find their way if they knew in which direction Gidon lay and they had a compass?" said Trevor knowledgeably.

"No!" said Manovra. "There is a magnetic field underneath the floor, which would send any compass needle spinning. Now, before I show you the way to Gidon, I must warn you about Sclarvete."

"Sclarvete? What's that?" asked Suki.

"Not what, *who*," emphasised Manovra. "Sclarvete is a Night Witch and Shape Shifter who looks like a very beautiful woman. She will do her utmost to prevent you gaining access to the Hall of Whispers. She will try and stop you from renewing the enchantment on the fountain of ice. Her powers were taken away from her and she was exiled from Gidon for enslaving the people of the Inner Earth. She was trying to gather as many as possible for an army to take over and rule here. Eventually, she wants to move onto the surface and your world. She is extremely dangerous and has the ability to change her form at will, into anything she chooses, animal, bird whatever. She also has the power of the compulsive eye."

"Compulsive eye? What's that?" asked Trevor.

"Quite simply it means she has the power of hypnosis."

"But, I thought you said she had her powers taken away from her," added Suki.

"Ah yes, she did, but Wisage our councillor gave her the chance to redeem herself. Every time the fountain of ice returns to its liquid form her powers return and she has the chance to pay penance and reform. So, she waits patiently until that time returns. Her first thought is of revenge, to destroy our kingdom by preventing the renewal of the enchantment and to wreak havoc in your earthly world."

"If she can change shape... how will we know if we meet her?" questioned Suki.

"One thing I can tell you is that when she dresses as herself, a Night Witch, she always wears red velvet and looks very glamorous. When she transforms herself, somewhere there will be a touch of that red velvet. Look

16

out for it. Now, my little ones, are you still prepared to help?"

Trevor and Suki studied each other and paused before both nodding determinedly.

"Here," said Manovra and placed what looked like a pottery pendant around Suki's neck which seemed to have three letters superimposed on each other, over an opalescent stone."

"IFS?" queried Suki.

"Innocence, friendship and secrecy. Wear it at all times. If you ever need help gaze into it as you did my ring and I will see and hear you." He turned to Trevor, "And you Trevor, take this." He gave the boy a penknife with twin blades. "Look into your penknife blades and you will see my image. You can always contact me and I you. Keep them safe and let no one else take them. It is a difficult journey to the Hall of Whispers and I cannot come with you. It is something you must do alone. Your penknife has a special quality. It has the magical ability to cut through anything. Use it wisely and well."

"Isn't there anything that can protect us from Sclarvete's great power?" asked Trevor.

"No, you must rely on your own skill to outwit her, but if you are by the fountain and you have a seven sided object between you and her, she will be unable to hurt you or affect you. It immediately sets up an invisible barrier between you. If things prove difficult I will send my own Magicat to help you."

"Magicat? What's that?" said Suki.

"Magicat is my assistant; a cat the size of a panther with special powers. She will be of great help to you should you need it."

"Cor!" exclaimed Trevor in amazement.

"Now, to show you the way to Gidon. Hold up your pendant, Suki. Trevor, hold up your knife."

As the children did so, the lumigles on the walls danced agitatedly and formed an arrow over one of the many passages leading off the main cavern.

"There," pointed Manovra, "There is the way to the land of Gidon and where you must begin your journey. Now, I must leave you. I will meet you again before the end of your quest. Remember do not believe everything you hear and see. Always be on your guard. Whenever you want to know the way, the lumigles will show you in the manner they did here in the Cave of the Shifting Sands. Farewell and good luck." As he said these last words he passed his left hand in front of him and vanished.

"But...!" exclaimed Suki.

"Cor!" repeated Trevor.

"Stop saying that! You sound like a crow!" giggled Suki as Trevor ran around her flapping his arms and cawing, "Caw, caw, caw!" He stopped suddenly and looked around him.

"He really has gone. Say, can you remember everything he said? All we've got to do?"

"I think so. We've got to somehow find this Hall of Whispers and put a kiss of innocence on the wall of the fountain of ice, join hands in friendship and swear secrecy."

"That sounds about right," said Trevor, "but nothing can help us against Sclarvete," he said despondently.

"Only if we meet her by the fountain of ice and then we need a seven sided object. Where are we going to get that?" groaned Suki.

"We could draw it on the floor."

"No, it has to be a real object. I told you to let us get some matches. We could have made a seven sided object with them," grumbled Suki.

"Well, we haven't got any, so that's that.... No! Wait!" Trevor added with a yell.

"Ooh! Don't make me jump," spluttered Suki.

"I've got one!" said Trevor with delight.

"Got what?

"A seven sided object. Here... in fact I've got two."

"Where?"

"Here, my fifty pence pieces, they've got seven sides... Count."

"That's lucky," sighed Suki. "Put them away safe."

"I've only got my pocket," said Trevor.

"Here, let me have one then, I can put it in my school purse. It's got a zip."

"All right, but if we don't have to use it, don't forget to give it back to me," said Trevor reluctantly.

By the time the children had finished their discussion they had moved around the cave several times and the lumigles no longer pointed the way.

"Which entrance do we use?" asked Trevor.

"We must hold the penknife and pendant up in the air like Manovra showed us, and then the lumigles will tell us the way," said Suki.

They both held up their magic gifts as Manovra had directed and a swirling cloud of bright lights seemed to shine out from them onto the wall. Silently, the little creatures gathered themselves together and formed an arrow pointing down a long rocky passage with a sandy floor. The children moved towards it and jumped into

the passage. As they did so, the arrow disintegrated
and returned to being little dancing lights.

Trevor and Suki moved warily along the passage,
not a word was spoken until they reached a fork in the
tunnel.

"Right, now which way do we go?"

"Ssh!" hissed Trevor I can hear something."

"What?"

"If you shut up and listen, you'll hear it, too."

Suki went quiet and strained her ears to listen. A low
mournful howl echoed through the passageway followed
by a whimpering and the sound of someone crying.

"That sounds awful. What is it?"

"How should I know? Do you think we ought to help? asked Trevor.

"I don't know, we've got a job to do, and besides it might be a trick."

"But, what if someone really needs help?" said Trevor. He had hardly finished speaking when a tiny little puppy came padding through the left hand fork of the tunnel. It was such a small scrap of a little thing that Suki let out a squeal of delight. It was Trevor's warning voice, which stopped her from scooping it up into her arms. Following on the heels of the puppy was a bent, old woman with eyes as bright and sharp as that of a bird. Her brown wrinkled face creased into a tired smile. She stopped and rubbed her aching back. Grunting loudly, she settled herself on the floor. Then she spoke. Her voice crackled like crisp dry leaves and she wiped a stray tear from her sparrow like eyes.

"At last! I can't believe it. I've found someone. Poochie and I have been wandering around these tunnels for weeks. Perhaps, you can help?"

"We will certainly try," said Suki, "What do you want?"

"I'm searching for Manovra and Gidon. My people, the fire people, need his help."

"Be careful!" warned Trevor, as Suki stepped nearer to the old lady.

The warning came too late, with the flash of a red petticoat, the old lady leapt to her feet and grabbed Suki's wrist. As she did so, a terrible laugh was heard and the old lady dissolved before Trevor's eyes and was transformed into a most beautiful woman, with

luxurious long dark hair and sharp scarlet fingernails. Trevor stood transfixed.

Sclarvete lifted her free hand and muttered something under her breath. A blue light shone from her fingertips and a wall of thorns and thistles twisted up from the ground separating Trevor from Suki. As the wall grew, Trevor noticed the cute little puppy changing into a small demon, gargoyle like figure. He heard the words.

"Come Evil-Imp. Away! Let us take Suki to our lair. Manovra's cause is lost." With that they vanished leaving Trevor struggling against the wall of thorns.

3: Separated

Trevor slumped to the ground in despair. He buried his head in his hands not knowing what to do. He sat there for some minutes but then he felt an inexplicable warmth spread through his body and a sudden feeling of wellbeing and calmness flooded over him. He looked up and saw a large, blue panther, cat-like creature, rubbing up against him. The cat spoke with a purring lilting voice,

"Worry not. I am Magicat and I have been sent to help you. We are to wait here until the arrival of Tweedikin. She will help us find Suki and we will complete your task together."

Nothing seemed to surprise Trevor anymore, not even a talking cat. He just accepted it all without question and sat in wait for who or whatever was Tweedikin. He didn't have long to wait. There was a rush of sound, a roaring wind and a thousand tiny sparkling lights, which swirled and twisted before his eyes. They settled together and started to take form.

Trevor could hardly suppress a little giggle of delight when he saw the completed form of Tweedikin in front of him.

There she stood in all her puffing glory; twenty-four inches of plump, perspiring fairy goblin. Her skirt was full and tweedy, almost like an open umbrella, set on six, stiff, white cambric petticoats, with a buttoned jerkin that was just too tight, and a small lace bonnet tied over her wispy, salt and pepper hair. Her rosy, apple cheeked face smiled down at Trevor as she propelled herself several feet into the air on wings that looked too tiny to support her very ample weight.

"So, you are the young man who needs my aid. Come on, get up! You should know better than to sit when a lady is standing."

Trevor scrambled gamely to his feet while Tweedikin buzzed around him, eyeing him carefully up and down.

Her voice reminded him of a schoolteacher he'd known in his reception year at school, a Miss Allen. Tweedikin's voice had the same efficiency and brusqueness.

"Not thinking quickly enough, are you, young man?"

"Pardon?"

"Your penknife, use it to cut through the thorns."

Trevor jolted himself back to reality. He took out his penknife and pushed it into the thorny wall. Immediately, the wall parted and vanished. Magicat, Trevor and Tweedikin set off down the passage hoping to find their way to Sclarvete's lair.

***

Sclavete struggled with Suki who had kicked and fought against her every step of the journey. Sclarvete stopped and screamed at her, "Little girl you can make this difficult or you can make it easy. I see that you have decided to make it difficult. I shall have to cast a spell to bind and imprison you, you bothersome child."

Sclarvete ripped off an ornate heavy metal belt embossed with duelling dragons from around her waist and cast it with a clatter to the ground.

"Wasted metal as you hit the floor,

Make me a crate with a padlocked door!"

There was a poof, a crack and a flash of blinding light as the belt exploded and transformed into a stout metal cage. Stunned, Suki shaded her eyes. Sclarvete's voice wobbled up the musical scale in an operatic wail and she pointed her talon-like finger at Suki who was instantly transported inside the cell. She landed unceremoniously with a bump on her bottom. Suki clasped the bars and pulled herself up before proceeding to shake them as if she could somehow rattle herself free.

Sclarvete strode on issuing her orders to her minion.

"Hurry, Evil-Imp. Drag the wretched child to our Spell Cave. Watch her carefully and *don't* let her escape. Or you will regret it!"

Evil-Imp grabbed one of the handles of the cage and tried to haul the prison crate, which screeched and scraped along the rocky floor showering him with blue sparks.

One of the sparks landed on his cloth jacket and began to smoulder and burn. Evil-Imp patted at the developing flame with his gnarled hand. He jumped about like a demented flea smacking the growing flame and then blew on it hard. It seemed to accelerate and then with a final puff it was extinguished leaving a singed moth-eaten looking hole on his sleeve.

Sclarvete's voice thundered back to them, "Put a spurt on and stop lagging behind!"

"Yes, Mistress," replied Evil-Imp feebly.

Evil-Imp removed his stout leather belt and tied it through one of the handles and hauled the crate behind him. It wasn't ideal, especially with his trousers falling down but it was better than trying to carry the awkward cage housing one small child.

Soon they reached a fork in the tunnel and Sclarvete magically initiated a moving platform, a travelator that would carry the trio toward Sclarvete's realm.

"Rocky floor no longer be,

A means of transport made for me.
Floor will move and ground will go,
Move us to my home below."

The ground changed to a flat escalator, just like at airports and moved them all toward Sclarvete's lair.

"Ahh!" Evil-Imp breathed a huge sigh of relief at being able to rest. He rubbed his red, sore hands where the belt had cut in.

They moved down through the rocks and earth, and twisting roots from plants. Suki sat staring in amazement at the passing, changing scenery. She frowned. She knew she had to get out of this. But how?

Evil-Imp replaced his belt and sighed in satisfaction. No sooner had he relaxed than Sclarvete batted him around the ears, "Now, pay attention. I just need to consult my crystal ball and we will away to Grushka's den. There you will need all your wits about you if we are to foil Manovra and his brats. Although, he'll find it tough with only one child to do his bidding."

The travelator stopped before a mystical rainbow shield that hid a kingdom with a red sky and crimson vegetation. An obsidian cliff stretched up and in the steep glass face could be seen a cave with a waterfall curtain that partially obscured it.

Sclarvete stepped forward to unlock her lair with a rainbow key. She commanded Evil-Imp, "Stay there and watch her. I need to know all that has transpired."

Sclarvete disappeared behind the liquid drape of water and vanished from their view.

Evil-Imp and Suki stared at each other, trying to weigh each other up. Suki, who had pressed her face against the bars to glare at the small demon, flopped back and sat back down burying her head in her knees.

Sclarvete, meanwhile, had entered her Spell Cave. An amazing amount of magical accoutrements littered the shelves. Persian rugs adorned the floor and splendidly ornate and carved furniture graced the spacious room.

Sclarvete crossed to a tall, ebony stand surrounded by gemstones and geodes. On the top stood a circular orb covered in a dense material.

Sclarvete removed the black cloth from her crystal ball and waved her hand across its surface.

"Not the future in this ball

Replay the past and tell me all."

Sclarvete watched and smirked as she learned Manovra's plans. She threw back her head and laughed wickedly, "He's got no chance! He'll have more luck finding a set of hen's teeth!"

Sclarvete rubbed her hands in glee,

"Now then, Manovra, let me see,

Crystal ball reveal to me,

What he does and where he is,

Flash, bang, wallop,

Show me his biz!"

Sclarvete paused, "Hmm, not a very good rhyme but it will do for now." She commanded the ball, "Show me!"

Clouds drifted across the glass and as soon as the fog cleared Sclarvete was able to watch in real time the events as they unfolded.

Manovra conversed with the Little People whose realm was in dire need of crystals. The land was bathed in darkness.

Manovra had broken off a part of the icicle crystal he had kept frozen by magic and installed it in the belly of the electrical circuit board.

There was a sudden transformation. A blue and yellow sun shone green rays on the earth. Birds sang and flew and the people clapped and cheered.

Manovra signalled Mergal their leader. He handed the rest of the crystal wand to him. "Here, take it. Go and heal the ill and ailing in your hospital. Mend broken limbs and bring health and happiness to your people once more."

Mergal bowed and scurried off intent on his healing mission.

Sclarvete still watched intently, "Oh, Shalutta! All these good deeds really make me puke. Still, no time to delay. I must get rid of this little problem brat. I don't want to destroy her that would be a waste. She could be useful as a slave or something." Sclarvete snapped her fingers, "Ah ha! I know just the person to help me."

Sclarvete replaced the cloth over her scrying tool and left her cave. She emerged through the water curtain and was annoyed to see both imp and child seemingly asleep.

"Evil-Imp!" screamed Sclarvete. "Let us away!"

Startled, Evil-Imp jumped up banging his head against the crate. Suki looked up forlornly and was amused to see an egg shaped lump forming on the little gargoyle's forehead.

Sclarvete waved her hand over the space between her and the cave entrance setting up an invisible force field that no one could see.

Briskly, Sclarvete magically transported them all to the home of Grushka, a Night Walker whose powers are strongest in the darkest hours.

"I don't have time to linger and I don't need you," sneered Sclarvete at Evil-Imp. "I have more important things to do. You will stay here until I return. *If,* I decide to return. The child is to remain in Grushka's cottage and you will keep guard outside her house but just for certainty, I will lock you all up with my rainbow key. For your own protection of course," sniggered Sclarvete.

Sclarvete muttered a magic spell under her breath, "Child sleep, sleep, sl-e-e-e-p." She snapped her fingers and Suki slumped into a spellbound slumber.

But Sclarvete was not finished. She pointed her finger at Suki and the crate.

"Fire, ice, cold and hot,

Crate and child defy me not.

Both will bend in time and space,

Transported to another place.

In Grushka's cottage you will go

For my pleasure, make it so."

There was a flash and a kerpow and a fizzing like a firework starting to ignite. Suki in her prison vanished from the ground to inside Grushka's cottage.

Sclarvete had succeeded in thrusting Suki, still imprisoned in her crate, and in a spellbound sleep, inside the quaint looking cottage.

Sclarvete entered Grushka's den and called out to the back of the old crone engrossed in some task, "Grushka, a gift for you. Have fun!"

Grushka was working in her kitchen laboratory. She dismissively snorted, and ignored Sclarvete. Sclarvete was unconcerned with this seeming lack of respect and passed through the cottage walls back outside where she set up an invisible force field around the house. Finally, she mused, "I think I'll have a little fun. I'll release the child from her sleep and the crate and she can annoy Grushka. That will give me great satisfaction." So, she returned to the cottage and opened the cage door. "Child awake!" Sclarvete snapped her fingers. Suki awoke and

gratefully took the opportunity to stretch her stiff limbs that had been cramped uncomfortably for so long.

"Don't think you'll get away, brat. You are safer with Grushka than you realise. You're doomed!" Sclarvete laughed arrogantly before vanishing into the air.

Suki looked curiously around her prison. She talked aloud to herself as she examined what seemed to be ordinary household objects. "Blimey, it's just like PC World or Currys."

A scratchy, creaky voice croaked out, "Ah! Another child. Let me see... Now, what do I need? ... Maybe a washing machine."

Suki turned around to see a bent old crone, dressed in black with her iron-grey hair scraped into a topknot on top of her head. Suki had thought that she was alone and jumped back in surprise. She collided with a vacuum cleaner at the side of the room and to her surprise she heard it speak.

"Oi! Watch what you're doing."

Suki stared in amazement as the vacuum cleaner started to whiz around the room, buzzing and whirring much to Grushka's annoyance.

"Stupid thing," screeched Grushka. "The spell didn't work properly and he won't shut up. If you're not careful," she threatened, "I'll unplug you and then what will you do?"

"Do you mean that this cleaner is alive?" gasped Suki.

"Yes, they all are. How else would I have all the gadgets of your earthly world? Now, leave me alone to look through my transformation book.... I think I'll turn you into a washing machine."

"Oh, no! I hate washing," grumbled Suki, who couldn't think of anything worse and she moved back towards the vacuum cleaner.

But Grushka had already forgotten her and had immersed herself in her book, "Now, let me see…"

Suki looked at the gadgets with renewed interest. She started to whisper to the vacuum cleaner, "Hsst! Tell me, were you once a child like me?"

"A long time ago on one of Sclarvete's visits to the surface I was stolen away. I was once a little boy and I never used to keep my room tidy. When Sclarvete tired of me she gave me to this old witch who turned me into a vacuum cleaner as a punishment for all my untidy ways. Now, whenever I see a speck of dirt or a bit of fluff I'm forced to go around and gobble it up. It's a terrible life but I've no hope of escape. Children never age here. My family and sister will all be dead now."

"What happened to all these others?" asked Suki.

"You see the fridge in the corner," hummed the cleaner, "He's a little boy from Australia who liked nothing better than to while away his time sunning himself and swimming in the sea. He used to sneak days off school and that's how he got caught. Grushka turned him into a fridge to pay him back for all his wrongs, he hates the cold."

"That's terrible!" muttered Suki, "What about the television set?"

"Oh, that's a little girl who did nothing but watch television all day, so Grushka turned her into a TV."

Suki pursed her lips and whispered, "Look, I've got to get out of here. Will you help me? If you do I promise I will ask Manovra to help you."

"What are you mumbling about? Can't you see I'm trying to concentrate," hissed Grushka.

Suki plonked herself on the floor as if in despair but really she was trying to formulate some sort of plan in order to get away. She whispered to the cleaner again, "Maybe someone is left... of your family. What's your name?"

"Bosworth, Charlie Bosworth."

Suki blurted out, "You were Miss Bosworth's brother?"

"Quiet!" screamed Grushka and pointed a finger at Suki, which zapped her with an electric current that fizzed and pulsed.

Suki twitched uncontrollably and painfully but she just managed to whisper to Charlie, "I've *got* to get out of here. If you help me I *promise* I'll get Manovra to help you."

"I would like to see Harold again."

"Who's Harold?"

"He's my brother. He hid under the bedclothes. But he couldn't escape Sclarvete who came as a red bird and trapped us with a net. Harold was a very talented musician and the last I heard was Sclarvete's personal assistant. I don't know what's happened to him now. He could be anywhere."

"Your sister became the gatekeeper to this realm," revealed Suki. "I bet she tried to find you."

"She almost did, too, a couple of times."

Grushka raised her wrinkled face and peered suspiciously at Suki and the vacuum cleaner. Suki slumped down and feigned dropping off to sleep and the vacuum cleaner buzzed off around the room.

But wily Grushka was not to be fooled. She scurried across, grabbed Suki and forced her back into the cage. However, she didn't lock Suki inside with magic but only latched the door.

4: Dangerous Passage

Trevor, Tweedikin and Magicat made their way as fast as they could in the direction of Sclarvete's lair. The rocky passageway they had been following suddenly opened out into a wild landscape reminiscent of the sort of terrain Trevor had seen depicted in books about earth's pre-history. He looked about him in awe. There was a sky with what appeared to be a burning hot sun beating down on swamplands but logic told Trevor that this could not be so. Was this another of Sclarvete's tricks?

"Where are we?"

"I don't know," fluttered Tweedikin, "I've never seen anything like this in any of my travels inside or outside Gidon."

"I have," mewed Magicat, "we are entering the mysterious and deadly Swamp of Despair."

"Swamp of Despair? What's that?" stuttered Trevor.

"It's a desperately sad and lonely place, where beings and creatures who have suffered are drawn into a marsh of misery from which they can never escape. There is only one safe path through the swamp, deviate from it in any way and you too will be dragged into the hell of permanent hopelessness. It is the purpose of

these things, these creatures, to draw in unsuspecting beings, anyone they can, to join the writhing mass of groaning misery you see before you."

"Where did it come from?" quizzed Tweedikin.

"It's another of Sclarvete's vile creations, anything to get back at Manovra and the dwellers of the Inner Earth."

"How do we get through?"

"Follow me, I know the path. But you must step exactly where I step. Your very life depends on it. They will try to grab at your ankles to pull you in. You must be steadfast and do everything I say."

Trevor and Tweedikin watched as Magicat started to weave a path through the treacherous swamp and wastelands. Everywhere the panther-like cat stepped, twisted arms and claw like hands reached out to pull her in to the hideous groaning mess of slime.

"Come on! You must take heart and be strong. Follow me."

Tweedikin sighed and flapped her little wings until they buzzed like a bee. She lifted herself up in the air and flew to safety on the other side. As she flew over the writhing mass of bodies, a terrible moaning and wailing arose from the swamp, rising to a crescendo. A hideous cacophony of mutilated sound echoed around them.

When Tweedikin landed there was something akin to a roar of anger, which filled the air and then dissipated into the sound of desolate anguish of souls in torment.

Trevor picked his way carefully, following in the steps of Magicat, but as each grasping hand came out of the mire to try and drag him in, he became more and more unnerved. The howling and pain filled shrieks filled his ears and disturbed his concentration. He nearly missed his footing and it was only Magicat's timely shout, which prevented disaster. But, the damage was done. Trevor stood frozen unable to move. The keening grew louder and the living, moving slime slithered around him. Sensing victory, a host of hate filled arms thrust upward and two terrifyingly gruesome hands clutched and plucked at his ankles. All was lost. Slowly and horribly Trevor began to be dragged into the living ooze.

There was a thunderous roar from Magicat and Tweedikin buzzed up and down dementedly at the edge of the swamp. There seemed to be nothing that anyone could do when suddenly as if from nowhere a strange figure leapt up and without any thought for himself ran along the partially hidden path, caught hold of Trevor's hands and tugged on them with all his might. Screams of anger reverberated in the air around the odd collection of travellers as the swamp's victim was whisked away to safety.

Trevor lay shaking amongst the leaves and debris at the fearsome edge. Magicat rubbed against the boy trying to inject a feeling of peace into the child. Tweedikin hummed and buzzed while the mysterious rescuer sat down in a crumpled heap on the ground.

When Trevor had recovered sufficiently from his ordeal he whispered his thanks to the stranger. It was only then that the motley companions looked, really looked, at Trevor's heroic rescuer.

Sat before them was a peculiar looking earth goblin. He was obviously far larger than ordinary earth goblins, who normally grew to no more than a height of thirty-six inches. His clothes were ill fitting and far too small. He had the largest feet that Trevor had ever seen. His face, which should have been round and happy, was long and sad. A single, lonely tear plopped silently onto the ground.

Politely, the group asked his name. With a mournful sigh the earth goblin muttered something inaudible.

41

Trevor asked again. But once more the words could not be heard. Tweedikin took charge and in her best school ma'am voice demanded that he speak up.

"I can't tell you. You'll only laugh."

"We won't. I promise we won't," assured Trevor.

Finally, one word was blurted out which stunned the group into silence. Trevor did his best to suppress a chuckle, which he hurriedly turned into a cough.

"Giggle who?"

"Giggleblue?"

"Gagglewets?"

"No! Giggletwinklesteps!" At last his name was revealed and everyone heard it was Giggletwinklesteps.

"See, I told you, you'd laugh," said Giggletwinklesteps.

"We're not laughing but you must admit that it is a very unusual name."

"I hate it. Everyone makes fun of me. Look at me. All other earth goblins are less than thirty-six inches tall. I'm more than sixty inches high. I'm a giant to them. They either run away or tease me. And look at my clothes. I can't get anything to fit me. No one wants to talk to me or be my friend, so I thought I'd come here and end it all in the Swamp of Despair."

A chorus of disapproving voices clamoured around Giggletwinklesteps. Finally, Magicat quietened everybody and said, "No! You must not do that. There is too much good in you to be wasted in the Swamp. Come with us. We are on a quest and when it is over my master Manovra may be able to help you."

"Will he be able to help all these poor lost souls trapped in this living hell?" asked Trevor.

"I don't know, but I'm sure he'll try." answered

Magicat. "Come on, we must get going if we are to save Suki."

After a little more persuasion Giggletwinklesteps decided to accompany the adventurers and once more the group set off on its way leaving the deadly swamp behind them. They made their way through the Vale of Mystery to walk onto Sclarvete's lair.

Trevor and his strange companions trekked through a green lush valley with strange birds and animals peeping at them through the foliage. Trevor stared in wonder at the many and varied creatures inhabiting the land. He saw multi-coloured chattering birds that soared in the sky and tiny deer only inches high.

Soon the path became more rocky and stony and led into a much more alien environment of weird-shaped rocks and boulders.

Together they picked their way across the unfamiliar ground, stumbled over the stones, and occasionally a wispy misty shape crept over a rock and watched them.

A feeling of uneasiness ran through the group who glanced back over their shoulders, every now and then. They sometimes caught a glimpse of a foggy shadow but could see nothing tangible in the coloured swirling mists that hovered around the rocks.

Before too long they reached the boundaries of the Land of the Night Witch marked by distinctive fire-stones and bubbling lava.

Magicat had led them towards a cave entrance with a waterfall drape. She announced, "This is Spell-Cave."

Trevor tried to enter but bounced back off the invisible shield. Tweedikin buzzed around in a frenzy before she puffed to a stop. "It's deserted. She's not here. Not Sclarvete, Evil-Imp... or Suki."

"And she's locked her dominion. None of us may enter." added Magicat.

"What do we do now?" questioned Trevor in disappointment.

Giggletwinklesteps offered, "Maybe she's taken her to Grushka's den."

"That's possible," agreed Tweedikin.

"Who's Grushka?" asked Trevor.

Magicat stepped forward, focused on Trevor and looked extremely serious. "Grushka's a Night Walker, a sort of witch. She's at her most powerful in the dark hours."

Tweedikin agreed, "She's one mean old mamma and is fascinated with man's world and the comforts it offers."

"She steals children for her own use and experiments," continued Magicat.

Trevor bit his lip nervously, "That's awful. If she's got Suki..."

"We have to find her," urged Magicat.

"That means we have to travel back through the Vale of Mystery. And that could be dangerous," warned Giggletwinklesteps.

"Why? Haven't we just come through there?" asked Trevor.

"The Vale of Mystery's harmless during certain hours, but in twilight the evil mists are at work," explained Magicat.

"Evil mists?"

"Yes. Deadly mists. We don't want to be trucked

with them. Many people have fallen foul of them never to return," added Tweedikin.

Giggletwinklestep elaborated some more. "They plant wicked thoughts in your head. Make you do things totally out of character."

"And the kinder you are, the better person you are, the more you're targeted," affirmed Tweedikin.

The group looked about them in despair uncertain what to do. Trevor piped up, "We must find Suki. We can't leave her to this horrible witch."

"It's not as simple as that," said Magicat. "We have to make a decision. Do we go onto Grushka's or wait for Sclarvete's return?"

They paused and gazed at the Land of the Night Witch. It was still deserted and eerily quiet. There was no way of entering Sclarvete's domain.

Tweedikin droned and fluttered around in a humming state of agitation. She appeared to go into a controlled hovering. Her thoughts seemed a million miles away and then she spoke decisively, "I say we go to Grushka's den."

Grushka pounded her wrinkled hand on the table and screeched, "Where are my spectacles?" She stared about her, first left, then right, before she fixed her eyes on the fridge. "I bet I left them in there after working on that freezing spell."

Grushka scurried to the refrigerator and tugged on the handle. It's stuck. She pulled again with all her might. "Darn kid. I knew he'd be a stubborn one."

On the lower half of the fridge door the bottom corners turned up into a sort of smile. Suki noticed this and couldn't help but grin too.

Grushka gave an almighty tug. The door opened easily and Grushka ended up on the floor with her skirts over her head revealing a pair of bright pink bloomers.

Suki seized the opportunity, opened the latch of her cage, and ran to the door, but it was bolted from the outside. She dashed to a window but every single one was covered with bars that were too close together for her to squeeze through, even if she could have opened the window, which she doubted.

"Thought you could escape, eh, little girl?"

Suki spun around to see Grushka standing behind her. The wicked old crone grabbed Suki by the arm digging her long, crooked fingernails into Suki's tender flesh. Suki squealed in pain and was dragged back and flung into the corner on the floor while Grushka mused what to do with her.

***

Trevor and his group looked about them despondently, uncertain what they should do, in spite of Tweedikin's emphatic announcement. Eventually, Trevor piped up, "We must find Suki. We can't leave her to this horrible witch. Tweedikin's right. We must go to this Grushka's place."

"It's not as simple as that. Other things are involved," said Magicat. "But, we do have to make a decision. Do we go on to Grushka's and risk our sanity or wait for Sclarvete's return?"

"But, she may not come back for a long time," murmured Giggletwinklesteps.

"I don't care what you say," said Trevor, "We have to do something!"

But, no one moved.

***

Suki sat back in the crate, with her knees once again tucked up under her chin. A stray tear tried to roll down her cheek but she stubbornly blinked it back and wiped her eyes. Things looked hopeless but she was not going to give the old crone the satisfaction of seeing her upset.

Grushka sat at the table with her book of spells, along with an assortment of items she felt she needed to cast a spell on Suki: a rat's tail, garlic powder, an eyeball, two slugs, a cup of worms, and a spider's web. Grushka turned another page in her parchment spell book and mumbled to herself. "Let me see... one rat's tail, garlic powder and the yarn from a black spider ... what am I missing?"

Grushka consulted her spell book once more, "Darn it! A nettle leaf from the Enchanted Wood." She wrinkled her already lined face and thought, "I may have one somewhere in my store. Let me think..."

Suki lifted her head sorrowfully but suddenly she smiled brightly. It was as if a light has been switched on by her cheery look. Grushka shivered, "Ugh! Someone is thinking pleasant thoughts. I hate that." The ancient Night Witch turned around and glared at Suki. "Hey, you! Wipe that grin off your face or I'll do it for you."

Suki stopped smiling instantly and Grushka returned to her book. As the old witch fell silent Suki raised her pendant Manovra had given her and gazed at the stone.

Suki gazed hard at the pendant. As she focused on the luminous stone, she began to see a faint image of Manovra. Suki's gaze became more intense. As it did, Manovra's image became clearer and clearer. Manovra looked up at Suki, aware that she was trying to contact him.

Suki instinctively turned her hand carefully, moving the pendant around like a camera so that Manovra could see her prison.

Manovra nodded wisely. He pointed to his ring and inclined his head again. He picked up a metal plate from the table where he stood and touched his ring to it. The metal plate slowly melted.

Suki barely contained her excitement as she realised what Manovra was telling her. She followed Manovra's lead and touched her ring to the rear side of the metal crate. The metal bars melted away.

Suki beamed with delight. She cupped her other hand over her mouth to avoid laughing out loud in pure glee.

The vacuum cleaner noticed and whirred around the room, as if picking up dust. It stopped by Suki, who whispered, "I need your help. Please, Charlie. Can you distract Grushka?"

The vacuum cleaner stopped to think as he tried to make a decision but he eventually murmured, "I'll do my best... Good luck, Suki."

"Thanks. I promise I won't forget you or the others."

Charlie the vacuum cleaner leaned slightly as if to nod in agreement then, once again, began to whir as he whisked around to the other side of the room.

The whirring sound became louder and Charlie squealed in a high-pitched hum as the vacuum sucked up one of the hag's old socks. The squeals became a grating whistling whine that irritated Grushka.

"What now? Can't you see I'm planning my spell?"

Grushka left the table and made her way to the vacuum cleaner. She caught hold of the electric flex and tried to follow it to the plug point and ended up crawling on all fours under the table.

Suki seized the opportunity and escaped from the crate.

She ran to the rear window of the cabin and placed her pendant on the window's bars to melt them. There was a poof and hiss as the bars turned white hot and began to dissolve.

Once the bars melted, Suki was able to carefully open the window and she wiggled half her body out and scrambled through the rest of the gap and tumbled into the ferns and grass that lay just below the rear window of Grushka's cottage. Suki stood and dusted herself down. She heard Grushka scream at the vacuum cleaner.

"I knew you didn't have the brains to make a good vacuum. I should've used that kid from Hawaii as a vacuum and made you into a toaster!"

Feeling sad for the little boy turned into a cleaner she vowed to come back and help them all before she ran off as fast as she could. But, came up short with a bump as she ran into the red aura-like force field around the cottage. Undeterred, she tried again to leave the grassy place but bounced back and was thrown violently to the ground. Realising that she couldn't escape she hid

behind the wood storage bin at the side of the house. There she sat and waited and thought.

***

Meanwhile, the daylight had dwindled and twilight was almost upon the unlikely travellers who moved cautiously from Sclarvete's lair and proceeded towards the Vale of Mystery.

Tweedikin buzzed and twitched, "I don't like this place. It makes my skin crawl. I feel like waving my magic wand and vanishing us through."

Magicat however reminded her, "We can't do that. We can only use magic if the children are in mortal danger."

"Like the Swamp of Despair?" asked Trevor.

"I didn't think quickly enough for that. Thank goodness for Gaggle Shank," muttered Tweedikin.

Trevor corrected her, "Giggletinkle..."

But he is interrupted by Giggletwinklesteps. "For heaven's sake! It's Giggletwinklesteps."

"Whatever."

The brave band carried on with their journey exchanging happy remarks, engaging in banter and chatter until they got deeper into the Vale of Mystery, where they all fell silent as the oppression of the place started to get to them.

Giggletwinklesteps face began to look even longer and more mournful and a scowl replaced Tweedikin's prim smile. Trevor walked uncertainly looking warily around as Magicat tried to stay focused on treading the right path out of the deadly place.

A red mist like figure peered over the top of a rock and watched them move along the path. Over another boulder a violet mist rose up and laughed silently.

Giggletwinklesteps stopped and yawned, "I'm feeling really tired. Can we just have a little rest? We haven't far to go now and my eyes feel so heavy and sleepy."

Magicat hesitated, "I don't know. We really should press on and get out of this abominable place."

Tweedikin responded, "I know we should, but I'm feeling sleepy, too." Tweedikin yawned and just as if she'd been shot in the back with an anaesthetic dart she slumped down by a rock and fell into a snoring sleep.

Magicat tried to stifle a yawn before she said, "Well, maybe, for just a little while..."

She rested her head on her paws, settled next to Tweedikin, and began a purring snore.

Trevor shook his head to try and stay awake but his eyelids began to feel heavy.

The red mist coiled around him and its writhing fingers plucked at him, drawing him down, down, down to the ground.

A red mist started to take form over Trevor's other shoulder. This mist tapped him there with its spirit fingers and it, too, whispered, enticed and taunted.

Giggletwinklesteps tried to force himself awake. He shook his head as if trying to clear it from a fog, "I'll stay on guard while you..."

The rest of his words were lost as he, too, began to slumber.

A blue mist enveloped him and a yellow mist engulfed Magicat and Tweedikin.

A green mist slipped over Trevor's shoulder and began to whisper temptingly in his ear. "Look... the others are sleeping. Now's your chance."

"Yes, why should you be bossed about? Who do they think they are?"

A violet mist played at Trevor's feet, twining, twisting and turning as it rose up his body. Its sibilant, hissing voice began its dastardly work. "Yes. You're the hero. You're the brave one."

The red mist added weight to the violet mist's words, "Think what you could do alone!"

The green mist coaxed and cajoled, "Oh, Trevor, if only you had Tweedikin's magic wand, think, think, think of what you could do."

The red mist tickled Trevor's nose as he slept and urged Trevor to leave; the words seeped into Trevor's subconscious. "You could save Suki."

All of the mists focused their attention and energy on Trevor. Their voices were mesmerising and the green mist continued, "You could be as powerful as Manovra."

The violet mist echoed sentiments already said and planted the thought, "You could do anything."

Finally, the green mist sensing victory called loudly, "Trevor, wake up. Wake up!"

Trevor came to and stared at his sleeping companions. The mists pressed home their advantage, "Look at them. They don't care," muttered the violet mist.

"They don't care about you or Suki," affirmed the red mist.

The green mist added more pressure and spat, "Go on. Take it. Take Tweedikin's wand." More tempting and enticing voices followed quickly.

"She'll never know."

"After all, you're only borrowing it."

"Borrowing it to do good. To save Suki."

"You can have Suki back in next to no time."

"And finish your quest."

"You'll be a hero."

The violet mist closed with, "Go on, take it."

A change came over Trevor. His eyes began to glow malevolently.

The mists hissed in glee as Trevor crept up on the unsuspecting Tweedikin and grabbed her magic wand. Trevor ran off victoriously and as the mists watched Trevor leave his friends they massed and swirled together before clumping and forming a huge black demon-like shape made up of specks with large red eyes.

They bayed together in triumph and then separated and began writhing around Giggletwinklesteps.

***

Outside Grushka's cottage, Suki studied her surroundings. She noticed Evil-Imp standing guard on the narrow path leading up to Grushka's front door and said quietly to herself. "Oh no, that's just great."

Suddenly, Suki sneezed. She tried to stifle the sneeze, but it happened too quickly. She hesitantly peeked around the corner of the wood storage bin and watched Evil-Imp.

Evil-Imp was startled when he heard the sneeze. He jumped in the air and spun around, checking out the grounds surrounding Grushka's cottage. Nervously, he walked towards the wood storage bin and called, "Come out... wherever you are! I'll find you."

Suki felt another tickling in her nose, she pressed her tongue against the roof of her mouth and pinched her nose tightly so that her eyes began to water. It seemed to do the trick but as soon as she let go of her nose without any warning, Suki sneezed again alerting Evil-Imp who rushed towards the wood storage bin. Suki attempted to flee, but, once again, she hit the force field. This time, it knocked her out cold and she fell backward onto the ground.

Evil-Imp gasped and ran to her side. He gently lifted Suki's head and cradled it in his arms. Speaking softly, "Little girl... little girl..." He lightly tapped his hand on her cheek and tried to rouse her. "Wake up... Suki... wake up."

Suki gradually came to and slowly opened her eyes. She glanced about her. Her eyes grew wide when she realized her head was in the arms of Evil-Imp. Suki was just about to let out a scream of terror when Evil-Imp quickly placed his hand over her mouth. "Shhh! You'll get us both in trouble."

Evil-Imp put his finger to his lips as a sign to be quiet before he gently moved his hand away from Suki's mouth. Suki was disturbed and confused, but not knowing what to make of the action she remained fearful and silent.

"That was quite a blow. Are you okay?"

Surprised at his tone, Suki rubbed her forehead.

She managed to croak out, "I think so." She looked at him questioningly as he took her hand and helped her to stand.

"Are you going to take me to Sclarvete?"

Evil-Imp looked down at the ground. It was clear he was uncomfortable, "I was supposed to keep you inside the cottage. I dozed off a minute and here you are. I'm in trouble either way... if I return you to Grushka, or take you to Sclarvete."

He folded his arms and rested his chin on one hand and thought aloud. "I'm doomed. Sclarvete hates me as it is, now she'll hate me even more."

But, I thought you were her favourite? Her right-hand man, as grown-ups say."

"Are you kidding? I used to be her personal musician. She liked me then. Until one day I played a song I'd learned a long time ago... I liked it, but she didn't..."

Suki interrupted Evil-Imp blurting out, "You mean you're...

... Harold?" and then she fell into unconsciousness.

5: Trevor's Disillusion

It was dawn in the Land of the Night Witch and the pink dusky hues spread across a pale azure sky. Trevor had run to a rocky outcrop with Tweedikin's wand. He jabbed in the air victoriously with it as if he was some sort of a champion. Filled with a powerful sense of being able to do anything he wanted he danced around in delight and shouted out, "I can have anything... riches, power, whatever I want."

His eyes settled on a humble grey pebble and he pointed the wand at it, and muttered to himself, "From what I understand all spells have to rhyme. So, let's have a go. Pity Miss Allen isn't watching then she'd see just what I can do." Trevor took a deep breath and announced carefully, "This pebble that I see. Turn it into gold for me."

Trevor stabbed at the pebble with the wand and it made a strange sound like an electric wire short-circuiting. It sent out a shower of iridescent blue sparks and a little puff of black smoke shot out.

He tried again. It still refused to work. Trevor threw the wand down in disgust and wandered off deeper into the alien terrain. His mood had changed and he was beginning to feel very despondent and guilty.

Back at the Vale of Mystery the mists had clumped around Giggletwinklesteps with their evil whispering, taunting, and whispering temptations.

"Just think what you could do if you could command the right sort of respect. People would listen to you. They wouldn't laugh at you and they would seek out your advice and your help..."

Giggletwinklesteps stirred as the words seeped into his subconscious but as the first light of day sent the sun's powerful rays onto the sleeping companions the mists began to dissolve and vanish, their influence diminished more with each passing second.

They washed away in their intense colour and retreated behind their boulders and could only watch what happened next. They had no power.

One by one the companions awoke and stretched. Giggletwinklesteps jumped up with a start and rubbed his eyes. He yawned loudly, "I just had the most awful dream."

Magicat looked towards him after she extended her paws and arched her back. She, too, roared out a yawn before speaking, "Where's Trevor?"

The others looked about them puzzled but they didn't see him. Then Tweedikin made a discovery. "My wand. It's gone!" She buzzed about angrily and spluttered, "It's the one my momma left me."

Giggletwinklesteps pulled himself up to his full height when a thought occurred to him, "You don't suppose... No, he wouldn't." But Magicat has already understood the implications of Giggletwinklesteps thoughts, "If you ask me, I'd say our young friend was tempted by the mists and stole your wand."

"It won't do him any good," blustered Tweedikin. "It's programmed only to work for me."

"Then he will now be feeling lost and miserable, and very guilty. We must find him... and fast," urged Magicat.

Tweedikin threw up her hands in horror and realisation. "If he reaches Grigg's Wood he's done for."

"Why? What's Grigg's Wood?" demanded Giggletwinklesteps.

"Grigg's Wood is inhabited by a fierce tribe of forest dwellers, the Sawney Beans. They like to eat children!" Tweedikin fluttered around in an agitated manner. "We have to find him!"

"What about the quest?" asked Giggletwinklesteps.

"There is no quest without Trevor or Suki and we haven't got either. Come on." Magicat bounded off followed by the others.

Tweedikin buzzed about looking for Trevor's footsteps to track. She spotted a dusty imprint and hummed excitedly, hovering over her find. "This way! This way!"

The group turned and followed her. The pale mists slid over the rock and laughed a baleful mournful hissing cry of derision and victory.

***

Dawn had grown into day and Grushka's cottage looked charming and inviting in the sunshine. Evil-Imp watched over Suki protectively as she slept. Suki began to wake up, stretching her arms and yawning. She blinked her eyes in the bright sunlight and rubbed the sleep from out of her eyes.

"I was beginning to wonder if you had a concussion, I didn't think you'd ever wake up," said Evil-Imp.

Suki looked confused, and held her hand on her forehead as to clear her mind. "What happened?"

"Don't you remember? You hit Sclarvete's force-field head-on."

Suki squinted her eyes, trying to recall the recent events and sort things out in her head. She thought hard for a moment before saying quietly, "I think I do remember. Are you really Harold?"

"Yes, but how'd you know my name?"

"I met your brother, Charlie."

Evil-Imp became excited, "Charlie! You saw Charlie?"

Suki nodded, but still rubbed her forehead. "Yes, but..."

Evil-Imp interrupted. "Where is he? We have to..."

Suki jabbed her thumb at the cottage, "In there!"

"What? Then what are we waiting for? Let's go!"

Suki put her hand on Evil-Imp's arm. "Wait...You don't understand. Grushka has turned Charlie into a vacuum cleaner."

Evil-Imp shook his head in disappointment. "That figures. He hated housework."

"Harold, if you help me, I think Manovra may be able to help both of you... and all the other children Sclarvete has stolen."

"You think he'd do that for us? After everything that's happened?"

Suki nodded vigorously, "Yes, yes, yes! He's a wise leader... a good leader... not evil. We can trust him."

"Tell me, what can I do?" queried Evil-Imp

"You're trusted by Sclarvete and Grushka. We have to find a way to get through this force-field and escape," urged Suki.

"Grushka only trusts me because of my connection with Sclarvete. She's heard of me but I've never met her face-to-face." Evil-Imp folded his arms disconsolately and leant his head on his hand again, and thought. "Hmmm... Let's see."

Suddenly, an idea occurred to him and he excitedly grabbed Suki's arm and jumped up and down. "I know! We need a rainbow key..." With that, Evil-Imp stood and ran towards Grushka's front door.

He turned back to Suki and indicated the wood storage bin, "Quickly now! Hide!"

Needing no second bidding Suki obeyed and returned to her former hiding spot. She crouched down behind the stack of wood and the water butt.

Evil-Imp raised himself up to his full two foot six inch height and authoritatively knocked on Grushka's front door, which creaked open.

Grushka stood in the doorway, irritated at the interruption. "Who are you? What are you doing here?"

The wizened old crone peered suspiciously in both directions either side of the door. She then glared at the misshapen being in front of her and her eyes narrowed.

"Sclarvete sent me."

"Sclarvete! Why should I believe you?"

Evil-Imp tugged at his red scarf around his neck and showed Grushka Sclarvete's emblem that all of her trusted followers wore. With more courage than he felt he stated boldly, "Sclarvete needs your help. Immediately."

Grushka's curiosity was more than aroused and she preened herself at what she smugly perceived as flattery. "Oh? So, she needs me. Hmmm! I figured this time would come, sooner or later. After all, I'm usually the one she uses to dump her useless little brats on."

Grushka pondered a little longer enjoying the moment and pulled at the long straggly grey whiskers on her chin. "What's she need? A place to dump you?" Grushka cackled raucously at her own wit. Her malicious squawk turned into a sinister laugh.

Evil-Imp maintained his polite stance, "No, Miss... Grushka. It's not that. She's growing some magical... poisonous plants. She needs rain water to make them grow properly, but..."

Grushka interrupted. "But, what? She can't follow the spell... her own spell, I might add... for producing rain?" Grushka cackled again, louder this time. The sound was like dry leaves being fed through a metal grater.

"No... She can follow it, but she's lost it."

"Lost it! And I'm supposed to make up for her mistakes?"

"Not exactly. She said if you help her this time, she'll give you half of the plants... they're very powerful. They can even make you invisible."

Suki cringed in her hiding place. She hoped Evil-Imp wasn't overdoing it.

Grushka thought over the offer for a moment, then poked her crooked, bony figure at him.

"All right. Tell her I want her to deliver them personally. Won't hurt her to eat some crow. There needs to be a little negotiating here."

Grushka stepped forward thoughtfully, "I must admit... I could produce a more powerful storm at night, but a calm summer-like rain will have to do."

Grushka raised her arms and spread them wide as she chanted. "Cold and clouds, wind and heat, clash and burst when you meet. Drench with rain the earth below, to make the poison plants to grow."

There was a thunderous crash from above, and rain began to fall.

Grushka slapped her knee with her hand in a self-congratulatory style. "Ha! Out did myself on that one... for a daytime spell. I've still got it! The old girl can still do the biz. Better go in and turn that little girl into a washing machine while I'm on a roll." With that, Grushka turned back and re-entered her cottage, and left Evil-Imp to stand in the rain. She firmly slammed the door shut then, it creaked open a crack. She called to Evil-Imp as he stood like a sentinel at the end of her front path.

"Tell Sclarvete I'll be waiting."

Evil-Imp nodded, vigorously. "Yes, Ma'am."

Grushka slammed the door once more and went back inside to her book of spells and charms.

Evil-Imp waited a minute to ensure the scratchy voiced witch wasn't going to come out again then, he ran to Suki. They both heard Grushka calling inside her home. "Oh, little gir-rl!"

"We haven't got long," murmured Evil-Imp. "Come on rain. Stop!"

As if the Gods were listening the rain stopped and a beautiful rainbow appeared in the sky. "Here we go," smiled Evil-Imp.

Suki gasped in wonder at the magnificent sight before them. The rainbow was made up of vibrant hues of red, orange, yellow, green, blue, indigo, and violet. Where the colours merged pink and purple hues banded together brighter than she had ever seen at home on earth. Butterflies darted in and out of the radiant shades.

"Now, watch this," instructed Evil-Imp as he pulled a red string from his pocket. "This is the only magic Sclarvete ever passed on to me. My magic... when it works, that is, doesn't last long. We must work quickly once they appear."

Suki looked puzzled, "Once what appears?"

"Rainbow steps, silly."

"Huh?"

"Evil-Imp carefully folded the rope in even increments, then suddenly pulled it straight. "Wheeee!"

At Evil-Imp's exclamation bright red steps unfolded down from the sky. They magically opened out from the arc of the rainbow.

Suki looked on amazed as Evil-Imp scampered up the steps.

"I'll be right back."

A beautiful young woman, Princess Gem, stood at the top of the steps, shimmering in a long, full gold and silver gown made of sparkling crystals. She looked radiant like an angel or as Suki imagined an angel would look.

Princess Gem held in her hand a large key made of all the colours of the rainbow.

Evil-Imp approached the majestic figure who spoke in a singsong voice, "I'm so pleased you found me, Harold. Now go... Go and help Suki and the others. I have been watching you. You still have a good heart. Your appearance belies what lies inside you, here." She gestured to her heart before handing the key to Evil-Imp who put one hand behind his back and formally bowed before her.

Princess Gem smiled beatifically as she watched Evil-Imp. He hurriedly descended the flight of enchanted stairs.

As quickly as they had appeared, the steps vanished, and Princess Gem and her rainbow faded from sight.

Evil-Imp and Suki hugged each other with delight.

They looked towards Grushka's cottage as they heard her shrieking angrily in a rasping, harsh voice. "Little girl... come out of your hiding spot right now! I *will* find you, and when I do..."

Evil-Imp wasted no time. He inserted the key into the force field and it dissolved with a flash and they raced away.

The odd couple stopped momentarily at the edge of the grassy yard. Several tunnels led away from the Night Walker's den.

"Which one? Which way do we go?" pleaded Suki.

Evil-Imp shivered before responding, "They're all dangerous... you choose."

Suki took a deep breath and with a measured tone showing more confidence than she felt, made a decision. "Okay... this one."

Suki pointed towards one of the tunnels. They both scooted into the passageway to temporary safety.

6: Fire Imps and Griggs Wood

Meanwhile, our other band of brave souls tramped on through the heat filled land that led to the fearsome but innocent looking Griggs Wood. The mountainside was a blaze of crimson, russet, amber, and all the colours of fire. Bushes burned but never seemed to be eaten up and Fire Imps danced.

As the travellers walked the smouldering path the Fire Imps shimmied out of their way and hid in holes. They popped inside the openings with little puffs of purple smoke.

Tweedikin hovered over the stony path that wound off towards the lush green Grigg's Wood. She spotted another print in the red dust. "This way! Look!"

Magicat stopped and sniffed a hole where a Fire Imp had hidden. A little spiral of hot smoke twined up and singed her nose. She shook her head and rubbed at her nose with her paws. "We're not here to harm you," she purred. "Have you seen a human boy about so high?" She indicated Trevor's height with her paws.

The Fire Imp jumped out of its hiding place. It resembled a little dancing flame and bobbed about pointing a flaring finger to the path that led to Grigg's Wood.

A shriek of delight erupted from Tweedikin as she spied something glowing and pulsing on the path. She picked it up. "My wand. I've found my wand!"

She shook it to test it. It spluttered and fizzed, whizzed and burped. There was a loud pop and Tweedikin was propelled backwards from the explosion. She got up and dusted herself down, then rubbed at the soot and smut on her face.

Giggletwinklesteps tried his hardest not to laugh at her, but didn't succeed very well. Tweedikin glared at him.

Tweedikin attempted once more to reawaken her wand's power. This time it sparked like a firework sending showers of fiery light everywhere. Some specks landed on Giggletwinklesteps and his clothes began to smoulder.

"Hey! Watch what you're doing," grumbled Giggletwinklesteps.

Tweedikin tried to rectify the damage, "Magic wand make him wet, douse the fire on Gigglesteps!"

"Giggle<u>twinkle</u>steps!" he corrected.

"Whatever. Just do it!"

A flash of blue shot out from the end of the wand and a large bucket of water loomed over Giggletwinklesteps' head and poured over him. He was soaked. As Giggletwinklesteps dripped miserably Tweedikin just burst out with laughter.

"Will you two stop playing?" remonstrated Magicat, "We have to move on."

As they continued along the path the Fire Imps bounced and bobbed about watching them; one of them was a pure bright red.

When the travellers disappeared up the rocky road to the woods, the red one dissolved and became Sclarvete.

She threw back her head and laughed in delight. "Go on. Oh, do go on! You won't get out of there alive."

In a swirl of colour and smoke she spun around and vanished.

The little Fire Imp who had encountered Magicat jumped up and down and said something to his friends who bounced and chattered. Amongst the foreign sounding words that they called, came "Goodbye" and "Good luck" uttered in their high-pitched fire crackly voices. The one little creature followed after the questors.

***

Suki and Evil-Imp raced on through the tunnel. Evil-Imp tripped on the uneven surface and took a nasty tumble, which sent him sprawling. His knee caught one of the craggy sharp rocks in the dank cavern. Suki stopped and helped him to his feet. Evil-Imp urged Suki, "Never mind about me, we must travel on. Quickly now."

They continued on their way, still running... but at a much slower pace than before. Evil-Imp rubbed his right knee as he ran. Blood seeped through his clothes and onto his hand. He grimaced but heroically he carried on regardless.

***

The other motley crew travelled the path to Grigg's Woods. Giggletwinklesteps, dismayed at being drenched with water, complained, "Just look at me... I'm soaked."

"Oh, hush. Would you rather have turned to charcoal?" returned Tweedikin.

"If you'd have been more careful, this never..."

Tweedikin raised her wand, "Oh, for heaven's sake... I'll dry you up."

"No way! I don't want that thing pointed at me again."

Magicat tired of their bickering roared, "Enough! You two are enabling Sclarvete to divide us."

Giggletwinklesteps and Tweedikin both jumped when Magicat roared. Tweedikin pirouetted involuntarily in the air and Giggletwinklesteps gawped at Magicat who had grabbed their full attention.

"We must rise above Sclarvete's evil ways. Good will always conquer evil ... in time. We are comrades on this quest. We must draw on the strength of our true friendship to help us through. This constant sniping is playing right into her hands."

Tweedikin and Giggletwinklesteps' faces softened. Tweedikin placed her hand on Giggletwinklesteps' drenched shoulder, then quickly withdrew it and wiped it on her skirt.

"I'm sorry, Gigglestick. I really only meant to help you."

Giggletwinklesteps flashed a sheepish grin at Tweedikin.

"I know you did." Giggletwinklesteps paused a moment, then... "By the way... it's Giggletwinklesteps!"

Tweedikin looked at Giggletwinklesteps, and then at Magicat. Suddenly, they all burst into laughter, friendly laughter.

Tweedikin hugged Giggletwinklesteps. When she stepped back, she, too, was soaked. She held her arms out and looked down at her wet clothes. Once again, the three friends shared a good laugh.

Magicat broke the merriment, "I've been thinking."

"That's what the noise was!" gurgled Giggletwinklesteps.

"No, seriously. Part of your problem is your name."

"It is kind of ridiculous," he responded.

"If you feel silly, and think it's silly, other people will think it's silly."

Tweedikin added, "I don't know what your parents were thinking of... calling you Twinkletoes with feet like yours!"

"Giggle... twinkle... steps!" emphasised the Earth Goblin.

"That's even worse," muttered Tweedikin.

"But what can I do?"

"You need a new name," affirmed Magicat.

The three friends solemnly marched on, lost in thought, until they finally reached the edge of Grigg's Wood.

Magicat suddenly held up her paw to silence the others.

"We must be silent now... we are entering Grigg's Wood."

***

Suki and Evil-Imp neared the end of the tunnel. Evil-Imp stopped, his breathing was ragged, "Finally, at last … Oh-oh…" he muttered cautiously.

"Oh-oh, what?"

"Oh-oh, Grigg's Wood; that's what. The most dangerous place in Gidon."

They paused and reflected a moment on what lay ahead and then proceeded walking side-by-side as they cautiously stepped out from the tunnel and faced a lush green broccoli topped forest.

They both winced as their eyes adjusted to the bright but glaring sunlight.

"It *looks* like a nice place, said Suki."

"Don't let the beauty of the forest fool you. A tribe of cannibals… the Native Sawney Bean Men… live here."

Suki gulped and her eyes grew wide with fear, "Cannibals?"

Evil-Imp slowly nodded his head up and down; "They wouldn't eat me… at least not in this form." He added quietly, "They only eat children."

Suki looked terrified.

***

Trevor wandered through the leafy green trees on the other side of Grigg's Wood. He stumbled along the path in abject misery and guilt.

Eyes watched him.

Native Sawney Bean men dressed in earth colours of green, ochre and brown, darted between the trees and watched the intruder daring to trespass into their world.

Meanwhile, Suki and Evil-Imp entered the east side of the dense Grigg's Wood forest in the opposite direction from Trevor who had arrived in the West.

The forest floor was covered with leaves, detritus and pine needles. Suki and Evil-Imp silently followed a twisting path that led through the centre of the trees.

A branch on the ground near Suki snapped.

Suki quickly turned towards the noise, and caught a glimpse of a native as he scurried behind a broad tree trunk.

Evil-Imp's head snapped round and he too caught sight of the cannibal. "Run, Suki... run!"

Suki and Evil-Imp fled from the area as if being chased by the demons of hell. Evil-Imp skipped on one leg every now and then, favouring his left knee.

***

Finally, Magicat, Tweedikin and Giggletwinklesteps cautiously entered the forest. A bird flew off through the underbrush. Its shrill cry startled them so they continued with trepidation through the woods.

The little Fire Imp overtook and passed them without being seen by the friends. He picked up Trevor's tracks and followed after the boy.

It was now dusk and daylight was quickly fading. The shafts of sunlight diminished and now the forest was a very dark place and with the darkness a sinister evil seemed to pervade the area.

Sclarvete, now a bobcat type creature, with extra-long red claws and a red gem-studded collar, watched all of the questors from a thick branch protruding from a tall tree. She purred with satisfaction. "The fools. The stupid, stupid fools. It won't be long now." Sclarvete's purr turned to a mighty roar.

As night continued to fall sending its inky black tendrils into every corner Suki and Evil-Imp frantically looked for a safe resting place, somewhere they could hide and feel protected. They stopped suddenly and stared towards the tree in the middle of the forest from where Sclarvete's roar could be heard that was still resonating throughout Grigg's Wood.

***

Trevor slumped down onto the ground feeling miserable and guilty. What had he done? He rested against a tree trunk. Startled, he leapt to his feet when Sclarvete's growl echoed through the now threatening wood.

The little Fire Imp shivered at the menacing noise and quivered, and then, even more determinedly, bounced off to find Trevor.

***

Magicat, Tweedikin, and Giggletwinklesteps continued to wind their way through the closely-knit trees. Each one looked up towards Sclarvete's resting tree as the eerie sound of her cry permeated the heavy night air.

Magicat whispered to his travelling companions, "I don't like the sound of that."

***

Trevor found a spot underneath a sprawling bush that he felt would keep him hidden from sight and crawled into it. He pulled brushwood around him and settled down. In spite of the eerie sounds and cries resounding in the forest he was so tired that the strange noises faded from his mind and ears and he drifted off to sleep.

The following morning, Trevor awoke, yawned, and stretched. For a moment he wondered where he was and then the memory of what he'd done flooded back to him. He crawled out from under the bush, stood up and made for a clearing he could see in the distance. His heart was feeling like it would break and his pace was heavy and slow.

As Trevor entered the open space he was aware of a snort behind him. To his horror, he saw a number of raggedly dressed, wild looking men approaching him from behind. They carried primitive weapons and spears. Some of them wore knife and fork necklaces around their necks.

Trevor was rooted to the spot, his mouth shaped in an "o" of horror for the scream that never came.

With a screech of glee, the horde of men surrounded and captured him then tied him up with a creeping vine. Triumphantly jabbing their spears in the air, they dragged him off towards their village. Trevor didn't even cry out. He felt in some way that he deserved it, and regarded it as a punishment.

From out of the bushes popped the little Fire Imp who bobbed up and down. He was in a dilemma, should he follow Trevor or travel back to Magicat and friends? He decided to back track to Magicat and company, and flickered off.

***

Magicat, Tweedikin and Giggletwinklesteps each stretched and yawned, as they awoke from their slumber.

The distressed Fire Imp joined them from a path in the clearing, and tried to communicate what he's seen.

Magicat tilted her head to one side and pawed her whiskers as she listened to the spits, crackles, and fire noises.

Frustrated the blue panther turned to the others, "I don't understand him. Do you?"

Tweedikin buzzed around the tiny Imp and fluttered as she listened. She appeared to understand him as he repeated his warnings.

"Well? What did he say?" asked Magicat.

"I have no idea. I can't understand a word he says," puffed Tweedikin.

"Oh, for heavens sake! Can't you understand Fire Talk?" said Giggletwinklesteps to which, Magicat and Tweedikin chorused a resounding, "No!"

"Oh."

Exasperated Tweedikin blurted, "What does he say?"

"He's seen Trevor."

"Where?" asked Magicat urgently.

"Captured by the Sawney Bean Men."

"But, they'll eat him! Now, what do we do?" bumbled Tweedikin.

"We follow carefully, if the Imp's prepared to lead us," decided Magicat.

The little Fire Imp danced excitedly up and down.

"I'll take that as a 'yes,'" smiled Magicat.

7: Cannibal Village

The Sawney Bean Men dragged Trevor like a rag doll into their village.

The rest of the tribe came out jubilantly. Some curiously prodded and poked Trevor, feeling his flesh and making slurping noises. They rubbed their tummies in glee almost drooling as they eyed the young boy.

The women grabbed Trevor and tied him to a stake and began to gather brushwood for a fire. On top of this pyre sat a huge cast iron pot.

The women sang as they brought water to the pot and filled it. They threw in handfuls of herbs and garlic.

The song sounded like gibberish but one word could be heard occasionally, which made sense. It was "DINNER."

An elder tribesman took a fork and stabbed at Trevor to test his flesh. Trevor winced and his face filled with terror.

The tribe members came out in celebration and began to dance and sing delightedly around their captured prey. Suddenly, a bolt of blue lightning flashed in the sky.

The tribe members looked up in fear. As they did, they saw a woman sitting astride the lightning bolt, which transformed into a red-carpeted stairway. The woman was wearing a magnificent jewelled crown. She appeared at the top of the stairs. It was Sclarvete.

Sclarvete wore a crimson velvet gown, with a form-fitting bodice and long, full skirt. She held a sparkling scarlet wand and introduced herself in a forceful voice. "Behold, I am Queen of Gidon. You must do as I say."

The tribe members exchanged puzzled, fearful looks.

Sclarvete locked eyes with the Chief then pointed her wand directly at him. "Should you choose *not* to obey me, your tribe will be exterminated and replaced with my loyal followers."

Sclarvete waved her wand and zapped a tall tree. The Chief and his tribe members watched helplessly as the massive tree was completely uprooted and toppled to the ground.

The Chief remained perfectly still as he turned his eyes to his right, then to his left, and contemplated what to do. After a moment of silence, he nodded in obedience and bowed to Sclarvete.

"Wise decision," smirked Sclarvete. "Now... send your best hunters into the wood. They are to bring back a young girl and an Imp who are travelling together, and another group of travellers... a blue Panther, an Earth Goblin, and a Fairy Goblin. It shouldn't be too difficult a task... even for imbeciles."

Sclarvete aimed her wand at the sky and thunder boomed from behind the clouds. She then turned her attention back to the Chief. "Do it! Now!"

With that, Sclarvete waved her wand one last time. She and the stairs disappeared.

The Chief immediately shouted gibberish-sounding orders at his chosen tribesmen. They scattered into the wood, chanting more incomprehensible mutterings in deep voices.

***

Deep in the forest Suki and Evil-Imp lay flat on the ground, covered with leafy tree branches, in hiding. They were adequately camouflaged, with only parts of their faces exposed.

They heard Sclarvete's magical peal of thunder coming from the village and moved their heads slightly, and exchanged uneasy looks. As they did so, they heard the chanting of the tribesmen, and froze in position lying totally still. They heard thudding footsteps nearing them. Without warning, Suki broke the silence with a series of loud sneezes.

In another part of the wood two tribesmen dived back and forth, covering the ground between two clusters of trees. When Suki sneezed, the two men stopped. Together they sprinted in the direction of Suki and Evil-Imp.

Suki turned to Evil-Imp and whispered. "I'm sorry, Harold. The leaves made me sneeze!"

Kindly he responded, "That's okay... but we'd better find a new hiding place."

Suki and Evil-Imp rose and searched about them as they brushed themselves off.

"Which way?" asked a crestfallen Suki.

"They may have us surrounded." Evil-Imp pointed to an area dense with trees. "Let's try over there."

The two dashed off together. Evil-Imp was still in pain and favouring his left leg, which slowed them down. "It's no good, Suki. You go ahead without me, I'll only hold you back."

Suki took his arm to assist him. "No way... we're friends 'til the end, right!"

Evil-Imp grinned in relief, "Right."

The two tribesmen have now run back and forth between several trees searching the shrubbery, and have sneaked closer and closer to Suki and Evil-Imp, who were unaware of their pursuers and hadn't seen them.

The tribesmen pounced from behind two tall trees and easily ambushed and captured the slow-moving duo. Although the brave two struggled, they were soon overpowered by the men who then triumphantly hauled them back to their village holding them aloft in a victory pose.

Trevor was still tied to the stake. Suki and Evil-Imp were pulled to the same stake and bound to it on the other side.

Magicat, Tweedikin and Giggletwinklesteps watched, unobserved and in horror, from the shadow of the foliage. What could they do?

But, further into the forest Sclarvete, back in her tree perch as the Bobcat, waved a hand over her body and wove a magic spell. She incanted, "By the power of darkest night, fill me up with cruellest might. My nails as claws and talons be, my eyes the sharpest keenest see, feathers ruffle, feathers prowl, turn me into Tawny owl!"

There was a flash and crack of thunder as Sclarvete morphed into an owl with red eyes and red banded marking around her neck. She flapped her wings and flew through the forest seeking signs of the children and their companions.

In the village Suki and Evil-Imp were secured. The Sawney Bean Men chanted in triumph. One banged a drum.

Suki looking terrified hissed at Trevor, "Trevor! Where's your penknife?"

"In my back pocket."

"Can you reach it?"

"I'll try."

Trevor wriggled his hands and fingers and touched Evil-Imp's hand. He jumped.

"Well?"

"That Gargoyle thing's in the way."

"He's not a Gargoyle. He's Harold."

"What?

"No time to explain. Harold, can you reach Trevor's knife?"

Harold wiggled his bony fingers and prized them down into Trevor's pocket. He touched the handle and

struggled to lift it free. As he pulled it out it touched their bond and the ropes fell away.

"Now what?" asked Trevor.

The companions still watched from the bushes.

Tweedikin murmured, "I think they're loose."

"But it's not safe for them to run," whispered Magicat.

"What we need is a diversion," added Giggletwinklesteps.

Before anyone can stop him, Giggletwinklesteps dashed out from his hiding place and into the clearing. He shouted, "Stop!"

The Sawney Bean Men stopped and turned to stare at Giggletwinklesteps.

One of them, a fierce looking, ragged red bearded warrior gave a blood curdling roar and charged. The Earth Goblin neatly sidestepped him, stuck out his foot, and tripped him up. The native went sprawling in the earth and spat the twigs and dirt from his mouth as he rolled over and stood preparing to tackle the Earth Goblin once more.

Five more cannibals turned and attacked Giggletwinklesteps. They ended up in a heap on the grass and earth, a tangle of arms, legs and spears.

The Chief, so involved in his ritual, proceeded unaware of the ongoing fracas behind him. He moved ceremoniously and took a flame to the brushwood heap when he was startled by the commotion.

The Sawney Bean Men had ended up in something like a pile of tackled rugby footballers. Straggly hair had become entangled in belts and they all seemed to be stuck and attached to each other. Through this chaos the Fire Imp danced about, burning and singeing their bottoms.

Magicat bounded in with Tweedikin and up to the stake. She urged the children to follow her.

As they fled the area, Tweedikin turned and waved her wand at the cast iron pot of water balanced next to the stakes where the children were tied. "Iron pot and water within, turn upside down and drench these men!"

The pot rose in the air and hovered over the men, who looked on in horror. It then turned upside down and doused them with water. A hissing burst of steam rose from their bottoms.

At that moment Sclarvete, as the owl, flew into the forest and swooped down. She captured Evil-Imp by the seat of his pants and took off into the trees.

Suki explained Evil-Imp's real identity to the others, as helplessly they watched Sclarvete carry him away.

"We have to help him!" begged Suki.

"You want us to help Sclarvete's loyal assistant!" said Tweedikin in amazement.

"No! I mean... yes!"

Tweedikin flashed Suki a questioning look. The others waited for Suki's reply.

"He's really a boy! His name's Harold. Trust me... we have to help him escape from Sclarvete."

Tweedikin looked doubtful.

But Magicat added, "We do trust you, Suki. If you say we must help him, so be it."

Trevor nodded in agreement, and then Giggletwinklesteps assented.

After a moment, Tweedikin spoke. "Magicat's right. We're all in this together."

"Agreed?" asked Magicat.

The companions uttered in unison, "Agreed."

Trevor piped up shamefacedly, "Look everyone I'm so sorry. I never meant for anyone to get into trouble. I thought..."

"Tosh," said Magicat, "We know that it wasn't you. It was the Evil Mists at work."

"Evil Mists?" asked Suki.

"Long story," mumbled Trevor.

The Sawney Bean men were running around dementedly. Tweedikin raised her wand, "Day and night by sun or moon, let these cannibals be fooled. If they spot a child somewhere, they will think it is a bear." She waved her wand. As the tribesman spotted Trevor and Suki they lifted their hands in horror and ran for their lives.

"Nicely done," praised Magicat.

So, the group set off to find the Hall of Whispers, and to rescue Evil-Imp.

8: Journey to the Hall of Whispers and the Final Battle

The comrades eventually reached a clearing at the edge of Grigg's Wood. They now needed to choose the correct tunnel, leading to the Hall of Whispers. Magicat lifted her paw and pointed towards one of the tunnels. Suki raised her pendant and the lumigles formed an arrow on the cavern walls.

"This way." Magicat confidently padded ahead, as the group entered the tunnel.

Magicat turned and walked backwards, facing the others as she talked. "When we reach the Hall of Whispers, we must stay focused. The Whispers will go to great lengths to undermine our mission."

Giggletwinklesteps chuckled, "I'm not afraid of a whisper!"

"Don't underestimate them. Remember the Mists. If we work together as a team, our strength will be great."

A red flower sprouted out from a crack in the tunnel wall and gave off a beautiful perfume, which tantalised Suki. The aroma tickled her nose. It beckoned her and called her and she unthinkingly moved towards it, mesmerised. "Look! It's beautiful!"

Before anyone could stop her she felt compelled to pick the bloom.

The others cried out together, "Suki, noooo!"

But it was too late. Suki plucked the flower and water seeped through the crack.

The crack began growing wider and longer. More water poured in.

The group started to run, while Tweedikin buzzed above them.

"I knew it. Sclarvete's trying to flood us out. I'm getting a little tired of her."

Sclarvete, now a lynx with a red scarf around her neck, appeared on a ledge in the tunnel before the group. She held Evil-Imp on a collar and lead. "Not as tired as I am of you! Run if you like, you won't escape."

Sclarvete howled, revealing wicked wolfish teeth and cruelly shoved Evil-Imp off the ledge. As he fell she vanished leaving behind a red cloud of smoke. Evil-Imp crashed painfully onto the rocky floor. He hit his damaged knee again.

Magicat urged everyone, "Run, quickly. We can beat the waters."

But, Evil-Imp was hardly able to walk, let alone run. He limped on gamely, but the pain in his leg was too great. He rubbed his injured limb as he attempted to keep up with the others.

Suki grabbed Trevor's arm and they slowed down to wait for Evil-Imp.

"We can't leave him," cried Suki.

"It's no good. I can't keep up. Save yourselves. Go ahead with the others," pleaded Evil-Imp bravely.

Trevor and Suki looked back but the water was

swirling terrifyingly, filling the tunnel. It was fast becoming a river.

"Hurry... everyone!" shouted Magicat.

"But, Harold has an injured knee he can't keep up," cried Suki. "And I can't swim."

Magicat stopped, and addressed the others, still keeping his eye on the advancing waters. "Harold can ride on my back."

Without hesitation, Giggletwinklesteps lifted Evil-Imp onto Magicat's back. The group continued running, while Tweedikin hovered over them, trying several spells to prevent a flood.

"Seeping waters, flow no more, seep into the tunnel's floor!"

Nothing happened.

"Darn! My grandma had a spell for flooding waters... I just can't remember it."

Tweedikin buzzed and scrunched her face as she thought.

"Wind and sand, now must meet, to keep these waters from our feet."

A slight wind blew and a bag of sand appeared on the tunnel's floor.

Tweedikin was delighted, "I'm on the right track!"

She pondered again and buzzed even louder as she flew above her friends. "Got it! I think. Gale-force winds and dune-like sand, stop these waters flooding the land."

A tornado-like whirlwind twisted in the passageway. For a moment the friends believed that the wind would die out and the waters would begin to gain on them once more but the fierce force began to gather speed and shrieked like a banshee. Suki shivered then squealed in delight and clapped her hands. The wind drove back the churning waters and a sand-hill appeared between the group and the raging torrent.

The comrades stopped running to catch their breath.

"Thank goodness... I couldn't run for much longer," heaved Giggletwinklesteps panting hard.

The other members of the group each shouted their thanks and praised Tweedikin who curtseyed in delight. "My pleasure."

The friends stoically travelled on.

Giggletwinklesteps lifted Evil-Imp from Magicat's back. "My turn. I'll carry him now."

Giggletwinklesteps pulled Evil-Imp up to give him a piggy- back ride to the end of the tunnel.

A few minutes later, the group faced the huge domed chamber known as the Hall of Whispers.

They stood in silent awe at the large craggy cavern with sharp rocky walls and cathedral type ceiling. There was one brick in the stone fountain wall with red threads running through it. Suki looked at it suspiciously.

The fountain sprayed out and the splashing water sounded soothing but underneath a hint of whispering voices could be heard. Odd mocking phrases drifted around them. Some words were clearly audible while others sounded threatening. Soon the infernal sibilant chatter began to penetrate their ears and heads.

"She will win, you will lose."

"What can you do? You're only a child!"

"You dare to trespass here? Do so at your peril."

Nevertheless, the travellers tentatively but with resolve entered the eerie Hall of Whispers.

Evil-Imp slid off Giggletwinklesteps' back.

Magicat announced, "We can do no more. We must leave you here. The quest is to be completed by you two, alone."

"But, what if something goes wrong?"

"Have faith, Trevor. I'll work a little magic here," promised Tweedikin.

"No! They must manage alone," insisted Magicat.

"Surely, something unrelated to the quest can't hurt?" implored Tweedikin.

Magicat reluctantly gave permission, "Very well."

The whispers began to grow louder.

"But hurry. We must go," pressed Magicat urgently.

Tweedikin raised her wand, "These two children standing here, take away their doubts and fear. Whatever they say, whatever they do, keep them safe and good and true." Tweedikin waved her wand but it just fizzed and burped. She shook it as it seemed to short circuit. "Darn thing. What's up with it, now?"

As Tweedikin shook her wand and grumbled, the red veins in the brick began to move and threaded out and formed into Sclarvete.

Suki shrieked. "Noooo!"

Sclarvete threw back her head and lifted her hand. Electricity pulsed from her palm directly at Tweedikin who was blown off her feet and exploded back into the tunnel.

Giggletwinklesteps rushed forward to help her up and then started into the cave himself in a fury of anger. He rushed at Sclarvete who sneered in disdain and spiralled her index finger at the approaching Earth Goblin who began to shrink.

Trevor yelled at Suki. "Quick! We have to do it now while she's distracted!"

Suki and Trevor rushed to the wall and kissed it in unison.

They shook hands and commenced the chant. "Hearts of fire, honest and true, together make this enchantment new."

The earth around them thundered and trembled. The whispers raised their voices in a cacophony of noisy accusations and warnings.

"Look out, Sclarvete."

"Watch your back, Sclarvete."

"Who's winning now?"

Sclarvete suddenly realized what the children were doing and stopped her shrinking action on Giggletwinklesteps who was now exactly the size an Earth Goblin should be. He scurried back to the safety of the tunnel to Magicat and Tweedikin where they watched helplessly and in horror at what happened next.

Sclarvete turned her wrath on the children, who ceased their incantation. Frozen to the spot they looked on in terror as Sclarvete began to change form into a terrifying red, fire-breathing dragon with hypnotic swirling eyes.

She thundered, "Try to outwit me, would you? We'll see about that."

Trevor, totally fascinated by Sclarvete's swirling eyes was rooted to the spot and could not do anything.

Suki suddenly alert yelled at Trevor. "Trevor, your coin. Use your coin!"

But, Trevor was unable to move or respond. His eyes were wide and glassy as if in a hypnotic trance.

In desperation Suki took her coin from her school purse and threw it down between Sclarvete and Trevor. A plume of purple smoke wisped up from the coin and into Sclarvete's eyes, which stopped them swirling. She began to cough and splutter and started to revert into her original form.

Trevor was able to move once more and Suki rushed across to grab his hand, which she held tightly.

Trevor tugged his coin from his pocket and held it aloft in his other hand between them and Sclarvete.

They started to chant again. Sclarvete roared in fury, her angry voice resounding through the Hall and tunnels. She began to morph into all of the shapes she had been in this incarnation.

The coins radiated energy, which Sclarvete could not penetrate with her magic.

"Hearts of fire, honest and true, together make this enchantment new. No more water, no more rain, turn this fountain to ice again."

The fountain began to freeze. A crisp, crackling was heard as the water transformed to icicles and ice.

"Nooo! I will not be beaten by mere children," screamed Sclarvete.

The whispering voices dropped to a frantic conspiratorial whisper.

"Manovra's here. What now?"

"Sclarvete has an hour left."

"One hour, Sclarvete. One hour."

The floor vibrated and Manovra appeared to face Sclarvete.

"Sclarvete! It's time. Face me and end it... or reform."

"I still have one hour, Manovra, before I lose my powers."

She shrieked, "Evil-Imp!"

The others watched in disbelief as Evil-Imp struggled to his feet and scampered awkwardly into the hall and bowed, "Mistress."

"Your magic lace. Now! Tie it to your finger."

Evil-Imp ferreted in his pocket and tugged out his red string and tied a knot.

Sclarvete tied the other end to her finger. "Magic mine to string you go. Through his veins my power will flow. When I'm but a woman plain, my power will work through him again."

Suki whispered, "What's she doing?"

"Sounds like she's putting her magic into the string and Evil-Imp, so she can use it when her power's gone," replied Trevor.

"Can she do that?"

Manovra stepped in front of Suki and Trevor, his arms outstretched, protecting them. "Yes. She has one hour left. You've fulfilled your part in saving Gidon. Run to safety... the final battle shall be mine to fight alone."

"But..." protested Trevor

"Now!" commanded Manovra.

Suki and Trevor obediently moved backwards and hurried to a hiding spot in a corner of the rocky cave.

Manovra stepped towards Sclarvete.

Sclarvete pulled her finger loose from the string, pointed her long scarlet fingernail at Manovra, and zapped him.

Manovra buckled forward in pain as his body was

sent flying backwards and he hit the wall of the cave and was left sprawling on the floor.

To everyone's surprise Evil-Imp seized the opportunity to run and joined Suki and Trevor.

Sclarvete turned furiously towards Evil-Imp. She lifted her finger and pointed it towards him.

Manovra scrambled up, raised himself to his full height, turned his hand and a beam of laser-like light shot out from his moonstone ring, which melted Sclarvete's fingernail.

Sclarvete howled dementedly and turned her attention back to Manovra. "We'll see who's the most powerful!"

Sclarvete held her finger up and stared earnestly at it.

Miraculously, her scarlet fingernail rejuvenated itself. She pointed it at Manovra once more.

Evil-Imp looked down at the red string tied to his finger. He threw it out like a yo-yo towards Sclarvete's finger.

Again, Sclarvete's fingernail shrivelled up as it melted.

A look of pure evil swept over Sclarvete's face. She no longer looked beautiful but cruel and evil as her true self showed through the veneer of glamour. Her skin turned red as she slowly inched towards Evil-Imp. Her voice was sounding more terrifying than ever before. She coldly declared, "How dare you use my powers against me!"

Trevor and Suki once realising Evil–Imp had not changed sides heroically positioned themselves in front of him to protect Evil-Imp from Sclarvete's magic.

"Out of my way you, you... hideous human... creatures!"

Sclarvete raised her hand again, but her finger was beginning to stiffen and turn to grey stone. She was unable to aim it at them.

"I warned you, Sclarvete. You can choose evil and turn back to stone or repent and do good ... and live."

"Never!"

As Sclarvete screamed out her answer, two more of her fingers turned to stone. She held them up and shrieked.

The Whispers murmured their warnings to Sclarvete.

"Manovra's strong."

"Sclarvete's weak."

"Maybe good will triumph over evil."

"Good will not triumph over me!" screamed Sclarvete in fury and frustration.

Sclarvete reared her head and tossed it one more time. She mustered up all the strength she could gather. She roared and turned into a magnificent lion with a shaggy mane, red claws and a scarlet diamond-studded collar.

Sclarvete, as the lion, leapt towards Manovra.

Manovra chanted, "Mevela, markala, zedo and brun. Rifula, stamu, traik and grun. This lion before us with mighty roar, shall be a kitten when touching the floor."

Manovra quickly ducked to one side and the lion landed on the floor of the cave... as an adorable kitten wearing a shiny red collar.

The kitten raced towards the fountain. As it ran, it began to turn back into Sclarvete as a young woman with raven hair and a red scarf around her neck.

Sclarvete's entire left arm had now turned to stone. "I will melt this ice. You'll see."

Sclarvete raised her right arm and attempted to point her sharp red fingernails at the fountain. This arm was stiffening.

One by one, her fingers became stone. Within moments, her entire right arm was completely transformed into grey rock.

Sclarvete collapsed in despair at the foot of the fountain into the same position as she was at the beginning.

"I thought she had an hour," murmured Trevor.

"That's true... an hour of Gidon time, not human time," explained Evil-Imp

Sclarvete's voice became low and grating as she desperately tried to move. Gradually she fell silent and turned completely to stone as the others watched.

The Whispers began again.

"She should've known... she couldn't win."

"Good will triumph."

"Evil always loses. Everyone knows that."

The Whispers, then subsided into silence.

The children and Evil-Imp scurried from their hiding spot towards Manovra. Magicat, Tweedikin, and Giggletwinklesteps joined them.

The group celebrated with cheering and laughter. Tweedikin buzzed happily above them.

***

A little while later, the group stood in the Cave of the Shifting Sands.

Trevor and Suki were swearing their oath of secrecy before their new friends. They stood facing Manovra, each holding up their right hand.

"Do you, Trevor and Suki, swear before me on this day to uphold an oath of secrecy regarding Gidon and its people?"

"We do."

"Do you promise to return to Gidon if summoned for assistance in the future?"

Trevor and Suki looked at each other and smiled. They then turned towards Manovra.

"We do."

Manovra reached out and shook each child's hand before hugging them. "You have my deepest gratitude for your unselfish service to Gidon and its people. We will forever be indebted to you."

Trevor and Suki paused a moment.

"You look concerned. Is something wrong?" questioned Manovra

"Well..." began Trevor.

"Please, let me help you. If I can, I will."

"Well... Suki and I were hoping you could help the children Grushka has turned into gadgets... and Harold. That's, if it's possible."

"Oh, my. Yes, yes. I see what you mean." Manovra held his chin in his hand as he pondered a moment. "Let's see... children, gadgets, Evil-Imp... hmmm..."

Trevor and Suki looked sad. They glanced at Evil-Imp, who had a tear running down his face, and walked towards him.

"I'm sorry, Harold," said Suki. "We couldn't have done any of this without you."

"That's okay. I didn't really expect..."

Manovra interrupted, "That's it!" Manovra looked into his moonstone ring. He could see Grushka sitting at her kitchen table and her "appliances" scattered throughout the cabin. Manovra motioned for Evil-Imp to stand before him. With Evil-Imp placed in front of Manovra and the image of Grushka's cabin and "appliances" in his ring, Manovra began his spell. "Vandar stir and blithers be, challow lark and withers cree. Appliances, gadgets and Evil-Imp, return to children with no limp. Let them all be happy and free, forever more where ere they be."

Evil-Imp reverted back into Harold. He jumped up and down with glee.

Through Manovra's ring, he saw the children... and noticed his brother. "Charlie! It's Charlie!"

Through the ring they saw Grushka throw up her hands in horror and dive under the table shaking in as the gadgets became children and danced around in glee.

Manovra attempted to calm Harold down. "I will take you to him. First, we must make sure Trevor and Suki travel home safely... before anyone notices they're gone."

The Lumigles glowed and danced along the ledges of the cavern.

The Little People excitedly burst into the cavern to join Manovra and the rest. Mergal was with them.

"Mergal, would you see that the children return home safely?"

Mergal bowed to Manovra, then to Trevor and Suki, "It would be an honour."

Suki took off her pendant, "Your pendant."

"And penknife," added Trevor removing it from his pocket.

"Keep them. Who knows when you will need them again? And this way we can stay in touch."

Mergal gestured to a coracle moored at the water's edge. The floor moved in a circular motion and stopped when the children were next to the craft.

Mergal motioned for them to step into the boat.

Trevor and Suki stopped and hugged Tweedikin, Magicat, Giggletwinklesteps, Harold, and Manovra once more.

Trevor beamed at Giggletwinklesteps, "Look at you! Sclarvete made you smaller like you wanted."

"Yeah... I guess it's the one thing she did right... but...I should be more careful about what I wish for." shrugged the Earth Goblin.

"You're not happy?"

"Well... I was beginning to like myself the way I was. My feet came in handy, and so did my size. It wasn't so bad after all... except for my clothes."

"If you like, I can change you back," offered Manovra.

"Really?.... But my people will still be the same. They won't change their attitude towards me."

"I have a better idea. Harold, your string."

Harold handed Manovra the red string, which Manovra cut into two pieces with a wave of his hand.

He handed one piece back to Harold, the other he gave to Giggletwinklesteps.

"What do I do with this?"

"Until you have really made up your mind... use the string. It will make you big or small as you wish."

"That's even better."

"Then it's done!"

"What about your name?" queried Tweedikin.

"It suits you, now you're small," said Suki.

"It does have a nice ring to it, doesn't it?"

"You could have a different name when you're big, like a superhero," added Trevor.

"What's a superhero?" asked Giggletwinklesteps.

"You!"

Everyone laughed. The children climbed into the boat with Mergal and waved good-bye to their new friends as they began their journey home.

Manovra stood before Giggletwinklesteps, teaching him a spell to use with his string.

Trevor and Suki watched from a distance as Giggletwinklesteps returned into his old "self."

Tweedikin hugged him.

She flew around in a frenzy as he shrunk again.

The boat started to spin.

***

Trevor and Suki stepped out from inside the grandfather clock. They carefully closed the clock's door and moved to the kitchen.

The door was no longer bolted. The children walked out into the bright sunlight.

Suki looked at Trevor. "I've got something for you."

"For me?"

Suki reached in her purse and pulled out Trevor's seven-sided coin. "I picked this up when Sclarvete wasn't looking."

Trevor pulled his coin from his pocket and reached for the coin in Suki's hand. "I never thought I'd say this, but you're not so bad after all... for a girl."

Trevor paused a moment, then... "Here... you keep it. You never know when you might need it again." Trevor handed the coin back to Suki. "Friends?"

"Friends."

Trevor and Suki both spat on their palms and shook hands.

The End

Also from Elizabeth Revill

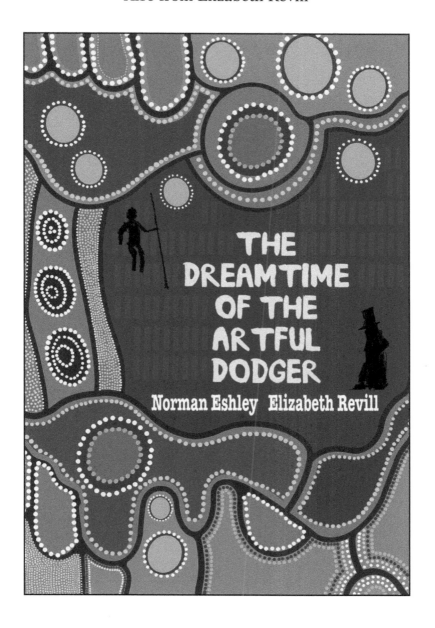

You may also enjoy...

AGATON SAX

AND THE CRIMINAL DOUBLES

Nils-Olof Franzén

Lightning Source UK Ltd.
Milton Keynes UK
UKHW020237240322
400505UK00006B/264